Entrée, Main and Deceit

Lucie De Havilland

Entrée, Main and Deceit
© Lucie De Havilland

National Library of Australia Cataloguing-in-Publication entry

Author: De Havilland, Lucie.

Title: Entrée, Main and Deceit / Lucie De Havilland.

ISBN: 9780987590107 (paperback)

Dewey Number: A823.4

Published with the assistance of www.inhousepublishing.com.au

Book One

Prologue

Remember these things Sass. Life, walking tall, confidence. The sky cleared and suddenly the wind was on her face, the sound of the ocean in her ears. The emptiness, isolation, serenity. This was her serenity. She remembered him now. He understood her when she thought, forever, that he never had. He had tried, he was aware, he knew she was complicated but he had loved her.

Remember Sass, the ring of happiness. She felt no more sorrow, no more self-pity now. She stood tall, said less, listened more. She remembered she had everything and many had nothing. She was happy, she understood that now. She wished he had known that.

Chapter One

I remember looking up and knowing, take a chance, make it happen because you are not spared, one day you will die. You are not special, well not that sort of immortal special. There are many different ways to live your life. Everyone has options. You can either sit on the fence, swinging your legs, watching, or you can jump. I was taught to jump.

Usually I type with such haste, I wonder why my fingers are lingering over the rolling waves, knowing what a farce it represents given what I actually know. I throw my head back at the absurdity of the situation, but knowing all too well how quickly the waves may roll on. Maybe I have met my match, maybe it is worth exploring given his words are more of a gesture than a voice.

Luckily we are all not writers, poets, journalists, philosophers. We are just storytellers and this will be told simply, like a true story should be told.

A slight beep from the screen beckons me back to the keyboard where my hands are still poised. A message, rather an annoyance. I know I will ignore it, like all the others. Yet what if, what if I actually indulge, take up the challenge. My mother's voice is quick in my head, "leave it well enough alone, you've done enough already".

She is probably right. What if though this time she's wrong, very wrong. Shutting down the screen I realise I need a distraction, Tomorrow I think. This cannot continue; tomorrow I will make a decision.

Chapter Two

It may be best to start from the beginning, like most good stories do. The marriages, the losses, the highlights, the deaths. I was the third child in a family of four. Mine was a middle class family with upper class dreams and upper class ideas. We lived at the end of our street, which began a fair way along at a moderately sized intersection. Our road meandered around a creek bed which flowed down over a hill, around a handful of bends, and then finally, some considerable way along, joined another street that bordered the State Reserve. We were at the end, four houses in. The charm of our street, which was often discussed between neighbours, was the large old trees that not so much paved the way like on Hollywood Boulevard, but rather featured spontaneously at points along the way, like monuments, grandparents standing tall, watching over the land. The street itself was delightfully wide, except for where at a blink of an eye it tapered in without notice and spun back out like a tape measure bursting free from the restraints of a long forgotten tiny waistline. Our house sat on a slightly elevated part of the street, nestled some distance back from the road and the front yard and the street ahead stretched out beyond us. The overgrown mess that encompassed our magical space made it almost impossible to walk through and the gate and fence were only barely visible peeping out through the sticks and foliage. No one ever removed it or cleared it away, and many people came and went.

I was born with a disability. Before I go any further, it wasn't an obvious one; I mean I had two arms and two legs and walked like everybody else. It was a hereditary disability, "in the genes" I was told. My problem was that I was born with the inability to accept things as they were or as everyone else saw them. Even as a baby, I cried when I should have been happy and laughed when I should have been sad. I walked when everyone else talked and talked when everyone else walked. As a toddler I was apparently nothing but troublesome and highly unpredictable. My mother told me it was genetic, inherited from my father who inherited it from his mother. My entire childhood was spent with my mother saying my life would have been far better off if I had actually been born with only one arm or one leg.

My father on the other hand thought I was a pure delight.

I knew from an early age that my mother was not my greatest fan and that the others were by far better. I was, well, the child who was always going to be sent back. My mother kept a letter on the top shelf of our pine wall unit. It dominated the lounge room, her handwriting scrawled across the front addressed to the County Orphanage always a reminder of where I could end up. There were times growing up when she had in fact convinced me someone else had given birth to me and what poor luck it was she had ended up with me.

Around the age of six I was finally escorted to the local police station. I had lost my mother's wallet somewhere in the freezer section at the supermarket and, always angry, she decided this was it, it was time I learnt my lesson. Out of the supermarket we headed, me being pulled along behind her and down the main street in the direction of the police station. My brothers and sisters were crying, tears streaming down their faces, pleading her not to take me in there, not to send me away, they would all help to make me a better person, teach me, show me. But my mother ignored them and told them to wait in the car. Walking away from our little white VW bug I could see their silent screams from inside the glass. I wish I had said something, like "See you when I'm older, when I get out, don't forget me." I walked tall, shoulders back, looking straight ahead, determined, brave and prepared. I had accepted my lot in the household and I sort of expected it to come; I was told often enough of not being wanted and funnily, as I approached the front steps of the oversized police station, I hoped that maybe this would fix me and finally, I could get some rest. After a talking to from the officer at the station and a wink from him to my mother, I was set free, confused but absolutely elated. Hugs and kisses came all round from my brothers and sisters when we returned home from the silent car ride and for the first time I felt like I fit in and wasn't the odd one out. The years of damage had been done. Our family was what it was. I grew up quickly and stayed out of everyone's way.

When my father was around the story was very different. The problem was that he was infrequently around and I learnt over the years how to prepare myself for the quick transition of two lives - life with my father and life with my mother. When I was eight my parents decided to split and for reasons I will never know, I was to go with my father and the rest of the family with my mother. Before I knew it we were on a plane, leaving, leaving behind my family and my precious little sister Brigitte. I was terribly confused. On the one hand I loved being with my father, invincible were the both of us together and embarking on an adventure of a lifetime. But on the other hand, if I didn't cause too much of a stir at home, life had been okay and the arrival of a new baby two years earlier had eased the way for me considerably. Nonetheless, the decision had been made and we arrived on new soil, warm soil in the dead of summer, early in the morning.

I was covered in sweat only by the time we had walked from the tarmac to the arrival lounge and dad was the same. What was this country, this heatwave? We moved in with a family, the father of a friend of dad's from their school-boy years whose family had moved not long after seventh grade. They had a bunch of children and a bunch of dogs and the house was cold and smelly, filled with old falling apart furniture and well-worn bedding. I knew better than to complain but the dogs' smell was everywhere and they ruled the house. We had never had dogs and I was terrified they would eat my feet off or bite my fingers.

The noisy boisterous household made it easy for me to get lost amongst it, and as people were coming and going I realised we were not the only ones to have taken anchorage here. My father was rarely there, he started a new job and joined the local golf club and when he wasn't at one of these, I guess he was simply out enjoying his new life; I slowly started to miss home, wondering if maybe it hadn't been as bad as I thought. Maybe it really wasn't so bad after all; what if I got what I deserved?

Coming home from school one Friday afternoon late in the year - almost six months from the day we had arrived - I walked up the front stairs of the house to the sun room. Looking in, I froze on the staircase. For what seemed like an eternity I stood there watching the people inside. Quickly I crouched down on the step, making sure no one could see me, trying to breathe slowly and calmly. I could hear the neighbour's phone ringing. It kept ringing as I crouched there on the rickety step. My mind drifted off, thinking about the phone call. Was someone trying to alert my dad that my mother had arrived, simply turned up here in a completely different country? The phone was still ringing and I was getting irritated in the heat. Tears started swelling in my eyes. Maybe my father knew she was coming but had forgotten or simply forgot to tell me? I felt myself standing then moving towards the room where my mother and my family were huddled. There was a jug of instant coffee and store-bought cake on the coffee table, both untouched. My mother was nervously folding and unfolding her hands, my babysitter swinging her legs back and forth and my siblings looking nervously around. The dogs were perched at the coffee table, tongues hanging long, ready for the crumbs of the cake. My mother was keeping her eyes off them but my brother was staring at them, eyes wide with fear. Tears were now pouring down my face as my mother looked up and then came to me. She held me in a tight embrace, her arms like the iron bars of a cell. She was crying, talking, between words sobbing, saying over and over how sorry she was. She asked me if I could I ever forgive her, and then said that she can't, so it doesn't matter.

What happened next is a bit of a blur because I passed out. I felt like I was falling, I had no idea why they were here. Were they picking me up or putting me down again? I was too overwhelmed, I couldn't hear my father. I felt exhausted. After years of living on the outer, of no affection, little touch, after years of being self-sufficient. After ten years of being an adult, when everyone saw a child. For two days I lay in bed. My mother kept vigil and when I awoke she swore there was a light in my eyes that she had seen in her own, the day I was born. It was her first reference to mothering me.

Everything changed after that. My mother, to everyone's surprise, decided to stay and before we knew it she had found a house to rent not far from the school I was attending. She enrolled the rest of the kids and I guess you can say we started the process of putting yet another life together. The time apart had strengthened and grown everyone. My position in the family changed considerably - not in an out of sight romantic kind of way, like the long lost sister with eternal powers - but something that sort of resembled what I assumed to be normalcy. I had at least become a sister and a daughter, sometimes struggling with the responsibility and sometimes struggling with the emotion. I had little experience in considering others or concerning myself with others and began to realise that being a part of a family was quite tiring and more difficult than it looked. I found there were times when I craved my previous existence of far less hassle, but never said anything. The road for all families is bumpy and more often than not the bumps turn into hurdles, which in turn transform into mountains, but you manage them knowing you have to in order to survive. I managed to come out the other side I think maybe even better off for the whole experience.

My mother is still an enigma to me. There is a relationship there, far better than what it was, but gone is the tenderness of our reunion. I can't be absolutely sure, I know many things will surface, cracks will appear and questions, millions of questions will be asked. I was still too young, incapable of handling the depth of the situation, not experienced enough to understand any damages done, so I moved on, moved forward with my life the only way I knew how: with my fingers and hands and feet crossed behind my back, just hoping for the best.

Chapter Three

We spent a great deal of time in airports in our new life. My mother had made a new home for herself and was keen to get the message back to all her family and friends about how well she was doing. For a long time I resented having to put on my Sunday best and drive for what seemed like for ever just to welcome some nobody who was apparently pivotal in our lives before we were even born.

"Let's go kids, Aunty Jade is on flight BA 219 from Canada and touching down in less than one hour!"

"Hey mum," I would try it on, "I don't recall an Aunty Jade, do you have a secret sister that you've been stashing away decade after decade or are we claiming someone else's aunty?"

"Oh Sass, it's just a figure of speech. Of course she's not your actual Aunty, she's Uncle Harry's niece's best friend from Vancouver passing through for the night. I told Uncle Harry we'd put her up."

"Uh-huh, pretty sure we don't have an Uncle Harry either Mum."

"He's your father's brother's best friend, now don't be so condescending. Get your sister and get in the car!"

It was hard to know if Mum was obsessed with being hospitable or concerned about being disposable or forgotten, but either way we were always going to the airport to meet, pick up or simply have coffee with someone whilst they waited for their connecting flight. At first the pure drag of it was relentless. Polite introductions followed by routine questions like that of a criminal investigation:

"Now who do we have here? What number are you? Haven't you grown?"

Occasionally someone sparked our interest; a C-list celebrity hockey player from back home; a gorgeous woman supporting a diamond ring the size of Mt Vesuvius (my mother's mother's next door neighbour's daughter); a lookalike Jesus of Nazareth straight en route home from some Kibbutz in the Middle East. But mainly it was the neighbour of someone's cousin, whose dog we use to feed when they went on their annual holiday. They were boring and loathsome.

There was however one benefit to our weekly visits to the airport: people-watching. Or as my sister would say, "Speculating on other people's lives because ours is so rubbish". For hours on end we would imagine the stories and create circumstances surrounding the strangers awaiting their arrivals, their impending reunions in the arrival lounge. Over the years the arrival lounge changed greatly. It started as a solid block wall safely hiding the contestants behind it, giving them sanctuary before stepping onto the stage; a moment to compose themselves, straighten their ties, apply their gloss. Then over time it changed into a tall, designer inspired wall, covered in art and scribbles that could make you dizzy if you had to face it for too long. It allowed a sneak preview of the incoming passengers – well, their footwear anyway, eliminating at least one question - and the fluorescent tubes that hung from the ceiling on thick metal chains, like in an interrogation room. From that it evolved into the modern era floor-to-ceiling glass automatic sliding doors securing nothing and exposing everything for the unsuspecting victims arriving after who knows how many hours of flying, jetlagged and weary. The scenarios and complex dramas that played out in our minds to provide depth to our characters never went unspoken and we would rapidly determine the scenes to unfold. My sister eventually found better things to do ("What," I thought, "could be better than this?") but I had remained faithful to the art. There seemed to be an endless stream of guests, many coming purely because they had heard of my mother's generous hospitality, some coming to see my father. His family would stay, sometimes not even seeing him, just using my mother for her home and hearth. My father ironically appeared as randomly as our houseguests, sometimes staying for a couple of days, sometimes just for a meal. It was difficult to be upset with my father because he was such a good-natured man, never judging, never demanding. Even my mother struggled, now that they were finally separated, to be terse with him. They became better friends than lovers. He would arrive always brimming with possibilities that we knew would never be realised. He played the guitar, sang, drank and entertained everyone and then, like a gypsy he would vanish. He had boyish good looks that like for the lucky ones got better with age, a Richard Gere type, and his looks saved him from many sticky situations. His attitude was no different, childlike, everything was a game. Every day he was going to make it rich, take the family overseas, buy us cars, expensive jewellery. Of course none of it ever happened. Just more music and more singing.

As I got older, friends along the way would fall in love with him, he would make them laugh and sing. I would always attempt to distract them and diffuse the situation. News of my charming father spread through my teen life, high school and then university years, giving me unabashed popularity. Girls I'd hardly spoken with would seek me out and invite me to attend some event or another, hopeful of maybe a catch up the following week at mine. It was peculiarly accepted amongst the community that even though my parents were separated (but never divorced, that was far too final for my father), he was still often in attendance with the family. At church, which was our Sunday morning chore, if he had shown up the Saturday night before he'd be there, patting everyone on the back, joking and laughing with all the other fathers. Looking back I realised we grew up with a healthy approach to dysfunctional families; ours anyway operated better with its dysfunction than without it. My eldest sister was the only one not convinced. She had seen the heartache my mother went through, she saw that none of us had a real father and she had no time for him or his entertaining, idealistic ways. He disappointed her with his many failed promises. I was the opposite; I was glad he was different. I knew other fathers who instilled fear and discipline, their children trembling at the sight of them. I was always relieved my father wasn't one of them. His easy-going ways meant he could interact effortlessly with anyone. He didn't require power or position. He told me that everyone was the same, treat them like they're the only person in the room, like they're the only one you can see and they will in return love you. Sometimes I would simply watch him, marvel at his techniques, and knowingly try to learn them. He was a maestro and he loved his audience. He had done it with us all our lives and he had done it with my mother for most of hers too.

It was no surprise to see later at his funeral that the church was full and the tears genuine. When the hearse had finally driven away, disappearing down the long drive way, the large mahogany coffin covered in yellow roses disappearing with it, the sting of tears and the echoes of torture that followed will stayed with me forever. I watched him lovingly for a lifetime and understood everyone's pain. I felt all of their pain on top of mine. I knew the man behind the performance. I held his secret, I had always been the one, the one he had really loved and maybe, but only maybe, more than himself; after all he had chosen me. I had his eyes, I had his smile, I had his soul and now I had his life. I knew that without him a huge void would walk alongside me for the rest of my life. I knew there would be no other, it was the bitter end of the person I once was. The man who saved me from ordinary, from poor expectations, from boredom, from loneliness. Without him I would have been like everybody else, I would have strived for nothing, I would be content with passable, I would not have considered the unthinkable. This man had invited me to walk the earth with him, me and only me.

The night before he died he tried calling to say goodbye, I later found out in a note. I remember seeing his number on the phone four times. I was out of earshot, too busy searching for what he had taught me to search for, life. So his call had gone unanswered and his final words never said. Now, on a good day, I take solace in the knowledge that he would have known, he would have understood, he would have even argued my case for me "Life was happening honey, you missed the calls. Don't beat yourself up". But the solace on a bad day drifts out to the ocean, like a message in a bottle. The regret is unspeakable and consuming and I find myself gingerly peering around corners, looking to see if the acceptance is there, only to find it's not.

Years later, I took my husband to meet him on the picturesque mountainside, headstones dotting the landscape through gravel roads and large old trees. The sun was ablaze and the sky was brilliant blue. My husband introduced himself to my father and assured him he would look after me now, that he would take over and keep me safe forever. He promised my father on that beautiful summer's day that it was his turn and to no longer worry. If my father had been able to speak he would have shaken his head and said "You will not, my dear fellow, sadly you will not."

Chapter Four

Not long after my 21st birthday I took the familiar route to the airport. This was my therapy when I was in need of some down time, a habit that just never died. I had just finished my final exam of the year - my final exam ever and I was free of my university life for good. I was elated and excited and keen to see the future. The airport had become my haven. It had simply stuck over the years. It was a place I genuinely loved to go to, never tiring of the hustle and bustle. Some did yoga, running, sport, stamp collecting. I did the arrival lounge. Friends over the years came along on various occasions but no one really got it. They had better things to do and would leave me to my bizarre hobby. So it became something that was for me and for me alone. My routine was to check the arrival times of aircrafts with at least half hour to land, giving me about an hour and a half before they actually arrived. This gave me ample time to assess the subjects and manipulate their stories. On this particular day, a flight arriving from Denpasar Airport Indonesia piqued my interest. The hot & humid weather outside with the threat of a downpour reminded me instantly of the one trip I had taken as a child with the family to Bali. My father had gone for work and my mother demanded we be included in one of his junkets. She was keen to go alone but the arrangements for all of us were too hard, so it was all or nothing. We had had a ball. It was the 'one happy family' memories of my early childhood.

Sitting in the airport and watching people come and I go, I saw that there was an aircraft landing at 1430hrs, giving me a good hour and half to relax and soak up the ambience. Grabbing a diet coke out of the fridge in the newsagency and pulling out my 'OMIGOD THE

STARS' magazine, I took a seat with a good vantage point of the lounge room. Singles and couples interested me the most, especially younger ones. Families were usually fairly predictable; an arriving relative, grandparents, aunties and uncles. It was an open and shut case. I had been that family on so many occasions growing up, I knew the ending. Oldies were never very inspiring either, obviously always there for someone younger. Looking around the arrival lounge I noticed the usual fare going on, nothing very interesting yet. I gazed out into the vast open space of the tarmac with the towers in the distance, the wings of planes littering the landscape, figure eight runways dotting the ground, small patches of green grass in between and eagles soaring through the sky. "I love this place," I thought again, "I love other people's lives."

Thinking back to the aircraft en route from Denpasar, I wondered what the weather was like that the passengers left behind, their holiday, their trip, the experience Bali gave them. I imagined the passengers, mostly tanned (as it's impossible not to brown up in Bali, unless you're a pom, or, if the trip was a quick one, spent secretly between bed sheets). I was expecting many families; Bali was a family destination as much as a singles destination. But did the families go for an escape, in the hope of rebuilding something they had lost or was it simply an annual event taken completely for granted? Were people attending a wedding – it was the third highest wedding destination in the world - or an indulgent birthday or perhaps an anniversary? Either way did it come up with the goods? Nudged out of my reprieve by the foot of a little girl walking through the seats, holding her Dad's hand, I looked up to find myself staring straight at the father. He was drop dead gorgeous and I couldn't help but stare. He was a Ken doll, tanned and tall, very tall - muscular and toned with blonde floppy hair, chiselled facial features and aqua eyes. He walked hunched, like he was trying to minimise himself into the little girl, a smirk on his face.

"He must be a model," I thought, there was no way someone that good looking couldn't be. As I watched him I was surprised at his lack of arrogance. He walked like he was unaware of his good looks, unaware that people were staring at him. He was the kind of man you might ordinarily overlook, except that he was a male model - perhaps even better. His serious tan seemed to indicate someone who spent a lot of time outdoors. "Maybe he's a swimwear model," I thought. "No, maybe he's a professional surfer or Ironman." He treated the girl with such a gentleness, like a child to a child, and interacted with ease around the tiny figure. As they took their seats he stretched out his long legs, leaning back in his chair and loosely crossing his ankles. There was something behind his smile though, a sadness, a loneliness. I realised the girl was not his; she didn't mirror him, like children of that age do when around the only people they knew day in and day out. They were close but not suffocatingly, anxiously. "Maybe she's his niece, or his granddaughter - or is that being harsh?" Giggling to myself I leant back in my seat, happy that college was over and I was completely free to perve on this gorgeous man, whomever he was. "Wow," I thought, "I could actually come here every day for the rest of my life if that's what I wanted to do, I could get a part time job and hang for the rest of it. Or even better, I could get a job here at the airport, then I could people watch all day long." The little girl dozed off in her seat, her head resting on the nook of the beautiful man's elbow. I wished, dreamily, that it was my head.

A mother and daughter wandered into the lounge and I watched them casually. Blinding diamonds on the mother's hand reflected off the light, shining through the large glass panels lining the arrival lounge. Her black square-rimmed reading glasses bobbed on the end of her nose. Mothers and daughters always share so many physical attributes. The mother was dressed from head to toe in crisp white linen, a pant and top set, generously flowing. The daughter -

differentiated only by her firm skin and youthfulness - was dressed stylishly in black pearls rather than diamonds. "This is a simple one," I thought. A husband and father arriving from Bali – the girl wouldn't tag along for an annoying brother or painful sister - and they are dressed to please with care and appropriateness. My imagination scrambled with endless possibilities and as usual I went straight for the jugular. Lies and deceit and deception. I truly believe there is a lot of deception that goes on in life. As I watched the mother she looked genuinely happy. Her eyes didn't give away the fear, anxiety and resignation I saw in so many middle-aged women's eyes. Maybe the husband returning was the real deal, legitimate. Maybe he's been providing some divine intervention in the region's archipelago. Before he arrives, the mother and daughter smile and laugh with each casually, chatting normally as mothers and daughters who are friends do. There is no sign of the distressed wife. Satisfied with the story of a missionary, his wife and daughter awaiting him eagerly, I was keen to check back in on Ken. As I looked over I was startled again by his savagely good looks. I could look at him all day. Struggling to imagine who they might be meeting, I try to focus. He wears no ring; not that that means much, he could still have a wife, girlfriend, boyfriend. "Maybe it's the little girl's mother arriving - his sister?" I thought.

My phone made a doorbell sound and there was a text message from my mother. "How did the exam go?" she wrote. I raised my eyebrows in surprise. Mundane details and day-to-day events were not something my mother usually entertained and I was amazed that she even remembered. I wondered why I would have told her in the first place. It wasn't that our relationship hadn't progressed, it had, but it had its boundaries, which the other kids didn't have. We had reached an understanding and I was fine with that. I texted back: "fine but no Nobel Prize here tho." "Really!" she texted back and typically I ignored the sarcasm. I asked her how she was going. "very well" she replied, "thank you for asking." Proper and polite, that's my mother. Far from what I am. She even signs her emails to me "Mother", like a title, a position in a corporation. If you didn't know her you could be forgiven for the reference to the mother in Flowers in the Attic. I once asked her (foolishly) –

"Have we turned out as you would have expected?"

She replied "Yes, exactly as I expected." But nothing more.

I watched Ken reach into his pocket and pull out his phone. He opened the top and flipped it shut again. It was an old Nokia style or something like that, not a blackberry, not a mac or an iPhone. I assumed he checked the time, the movement was so quick, and I wonder if there was trepidation or pure excitement in his actions. His face gave nothing away. The little girl behaved perfectly beside him. She had a handbag full of My Little Pony's which she lined up on the seat. Kneeling on the ground, she played lovingly with them, her battery-powered sneakers flashing on and off like the lights of a plane approaching.

I thought back again to college, glad to be finished. I was so ready to start earning, to begin the dream of finally departing, not watching arrivals for a change. "Not Bali though," I thought as I glanced up at the monitor to read Berlin, Russia, Amsterdam. "Definitely Paris." Somewhere exciting. The lounge began to fill and people started taking seats, waiting for the plane to arrive. A large group of students took their place alongside me and a flock of backpackers wandered in, their bags larger than they could carry, maybe awaiting the arrival of their mates backpacking from Bali. I caught a glimpse of the mother and daughter from earlier. They were looking pretty bored, the chatter gone, ready to move on. Looking up to the arrival monitor I saw our flight was flashing "landed". The lady at the desk announced the arrival of British Airways from Denpasar and everyone started to move, the level of noise picking up. I knew there was still another twenty minutes at least before anyone appeared, but people started to gather around the automatic doors, craning their necks to see in. I didn't know how I didn't notice her earlier, but sitting in the corner was a young woman. She had glossy blonde hair cut in a perfect bob that sat on her shoulders. Her expression gave me the feeling that a lot sat on her shoulders. Her eyes were the colour of sea, green, the type you see on billboards advertising holiday destinations like Tahiti and Bora Bora. She looked distant, removed, intriguing. Her eyes were surely the gateway to her soul, exposing a rawness. Discreet gold studs pierced her ears and a slim gold bangle dangled from her fine wrist. I noticed a tattoo just above her ankle which seemed out of place. I tried to make it out. It looked like a symbol of some sort - perhaps Buddha? Her skirt was too long and it fell endlessly over the front of her foot, hiding the image. She was thin but not ghastly thin. Genetically thin - with envy I conceded that she wore it well. She had two books. One she was writing in and one she seemed to be taking notes from or reading from. Her writing book was plain but elegant, it had a worn brown leather cover with a spiral spine and was no larger than a travel diary. The other was hidden partially by her bag and was much larger with a hard red cover. Her bag had a clasp attached to it, with various plastic cat figurines dangling from it. Some were stretching, some were sitting, some were licking their paws. Perhaps the tattoo is a cat and not Buddha. Hopefully she will shift in her seat again. If she had makeup on you couldn't tell, her skin looked perfect. Her blouse looked expensive, which was confusing, because I had taken her for more of a hippie or greenie. It was made beautifully of exquisite silk, the colour a mushroom pink with a high ruffled neck. Tiny fabric-covered buttons ran down the front of the blouse and the sleeves were short and ruffled to match the neckline. Her long skirt was khaki like her thongs. There was something so disturbing about her and at the same time breathless and timeless.

I remembered Ken. He was still sitting with the little girl, looking at the front gate. They could be a perfect match. The fever of the excitement picked up in the arrival lounge and the little girl packed her toy ponies back into their bag, their home. She held hands with Ken, neither smiling nor frowning, they didn't let go. He gazed down at her, his huge hand covering her little one and they stood in anticipation. The backpackers grew in size and noise and I moved a little to see Ken so excited to watch out the scene. I was once speaking to a backpacker at a nightclub who said most backpackers start out travelling on their own or with one other friend, before hooking up with other couples or smaller groups, to share and save costs for further travels. It was true of this group - everyone arriving knew everyone. There was a delightful Asian man, very well-presented, standing on his own rigid and proud. He looked nervous and I wondered if his wife or child was approaching. The lady with her crisp uniform and perfect bun behind the desk spoke into her desk mic again, wishing all the passengers either a safe holiday or a happy return home.

From where I sat I could still see Ken and his princess. Passengers were appearing in droves and started to spill out from the walkways, the mother and daughter were waving madly as a man in hibiscus flower shorts and a Pebble Beach golfing shirt appeared. He threw his arms loosely around the girls and kissed them both, all smiling. Following close on his heels was a boy, slightly older than the girl and carrying a golf bag. His mother embraced him and the father beamed. He pulled out a trophy from his bag; a gold golfer in full swing stands on a marble base. The mother was kissing and hugging him, and the daughter, trying not to appear too excited, grabbed her brother's trophy while giving him a soft punch in the arm. On reflection I realised a true missionary couldn't afford to clad his family in all that gear that preserved them.

Quickly I looked back to Ken, anxious not to lose him. He was still standing and watching. I was diverted to a lady coming down the hallway, she was being escorted or assisted – it was hard to tell - by two flight attendants, one on each arm. She was middle-aged, maybe forty, and dressed exquisitely in a Jackie Onassis-style black knee-length dress with matching strands of pearls around her neck and wrists and larger ones dotting each ear. Her platinum blonde hair was unkempt and dishevelled and fresh lipstick had been applied over smeared lipstick. Smudged mascara lined her eyes. She was either drunk or high or both, and the smell of perfume that engulfed her concealed nothing by arriving before her. The three of them headed purposefully toward the outer side of the arrival counter. Curiously I looked over in their direction, eager to see what had happened. An impeccably dressed and distinguished looking gentleman was deeply involved in punching buttons into his mobile phone. Slightly distracted, he looked up and then back to his phone. With a sudden jerking motion he looked up again, stunned. Opening his jacket he thrust his phone into the breast pocket and watched the lady, the look on his face changing. He stared and a quick look of recognition flicked across his face. Then his eyes darted from side to side in two very quick movements like he was surveying the area. Something close to relief flooded his face, and he made his move forward. The steward approached him and he was like an altar boy with hands over the holy cross, both of them knowing what it meant yet at a loss to understand sometimes why it helped. The tall man circled her with his arm and held her elbow tightly. He showed signs of concern and confusion. He shook the hands of the attendants, smiling broadly, and they hurried off down the corridor, pleased to be rid of the situation. Another man approached, also from the flight, and the husband smiled at him. I moved in a little closer, quick enough to see a fleeting look of panic pass over the husband's face. For the second time he outstretched his hand and they shook. Speaking quietly, the husband laughed a little and the friend left, gently touching the woman's arm, sympathetic almost. The husband escorted the wife quickly away, his arm wrapped firmly around her, his back straight and shoulders square. She stumbled a bit but tried to keep up. I was surprised to find myself feeling sorry for the lady and not the husband. Imagining it as a scene often played, I wondered why she was in Bali; it seemed a strange destination for such a woman. Curious, I checked the flight details again. From Korea via Bali. "That makes sense, a shopping holiday," I thought. Korea was famous for it. I figured that that was your typical marriage. Maybe sometimes it was the other way around, the man an alcoholic and the wife depressed. Too much sadness and too much torment, lies and deceit, a cage no one can surrender from. Who would want it, what a sentence! Children I understood, but one person for the rest of your life? That I didn't.

Before I realised it I'd lost sight of Ken. Panicking, I searched the room. Where was he? Looking furiously around - there seemed to be no sign of him, the crowds had thinned and if he was there I would have seen him. Rushing down the corridor and then the escalators, I bolted to the carousel baggage; hopeful he had only just wandered down there. Other arrivals were streaming in and by the time I'd located the carousel for the Bali flight, all that remained was a group of Asian students still tightly hugging each other, three bags going around and a round. Quickly I made for the exit, hoping that perhaps they were in the taxi line or still paying their parking ticket. I knew he would be impossible to miss if he was somewhere in the vicinity. But he was gone. Devastated and angry, I reprimanded myself for getting absorbed by the older lady. Even as I finally left I continued to scour the car park, hoping to catch a glimpse of him, maybe loading the car or still pushing the luggage. Nothing. I was miserable. Eventually I made my way to the car, deeply saddened by my loss. I couldn't stop thinking about him, the little girl, who they were picking up, why they were there and the abrupt realisation that I would never know. From time to time I still stop and think about him, wonder about him, my dream man from the day I finished college.

Driving out of the airport, the traffic was thick. Flicking through the radio stations I found nothing on and I turned it off, disgusted, losing myself to Ken again and then out of the corner of my eye I saw Mr and Mrs Heart leaning against a Mercedes, the problematic passenger and her endearing husband, but they had with them a girl probably about the same age as me, give or take a few years. She was putting the luggage in the boot while the man and lady talked at the open door on the passenger's side. She didn't look much better than when she had been escorted out of the airplane but now seemed to be arguing with him. He appeared nonplussed and assisted her into the seat. The girl finished with the luggage at the back of the car, looking out into the distance. She was surprisingly plain given her parent's good looks, but dressed equally as well. Finally, the husband and wife were in the car and the girl left her post at the boot moving slowly around to the back door. She looked weary and bored and she rolled her eyes as she got into the car. If only I had known we would all meet again, mother, father and daughter, perhaps then I would have paid much closer attention.

Chapter Five

I was born on the fourteenth of July, Bastille Day. A French national day, the storming of the Bastille Jail. I was born four weeks early, making me a Cancerian and not a Leo, and I was born in a town on the other side of the world, miles away from France in every possible way. Sasskia Catherine I was named, in honour of the date and my great great great half-French grandmother. It wasn't until I was much older that I learnt that, and still, even when I chose Genevieve as my confirmation name at eight years old I didn't consider a connection. The yearning to travel was in our blood. So much time spent at airports, watching thousands of people coming and going from around the globe, piqued all of our interests. My eldest sister, so fascinated, after finishing high school decided to study tourism at college. That was all the additional exposure we needed, as she coloured in maps of the world and sprawled posters of various continents and countries over the dining room table and kitchen floors. We would sit with her and ask constantly what country was this and what sea was that. The brochures that flooded the house as she tried to remember cities and attractions, pretending to be a travel agent to us younger kids, had been mind-boggling. I can remember them all now: the pictures, the photos, the people living the dream and loving life. I wanted to feel that more than the others I knew. When my sister succeeded in her studies of one country, keen to discard the paperwork, quick to get stuck into the next, I would ask for them, to store and pore over and wonder at.

Greece had captured me. The blue-green oceans on all the glossy brochures, my eyes bore into. I lined my bedroom walls with them, creating an oceanic landscape. You could see the sea from every corner of my room and I would fall to sleep on my yacht in the centre of the endless oceans, swaying lethargically from side to side. In a way the ocean was always, from the moment I woke up to the moment I went to sleep, somewhere in my mind. Even to this day, I can be driving through the busiest streets, darkened by the tallest sky-scrapers and can imagine the ocean is just on the other side, behind the next street. I can close my eyes and breathe in my childhood walls.

France was hot on my list of travel destinations, but intimidated by the language and the enormity of it all I went to the UK before it. My mind travelled frequently to France, through Champagne, Lyon & Provence, yet something prevented me from setting sail there first. I wanted it, but was scared of it in the same breath. I was afraid if I went, I may never return. It was like an illicit drug sitting on the coffee table at a grown-ups party. The attraction was suffocating and the consequences overwhelming. By the time I finally made it to Charles de Gaulle airport I knew I had been right all along and the yearning is now firmly entrenched in my bones. And so it was at 24, I went. My first real love, my French love.

Chapter Six

It was straight out of a textbook: he was married and by the time I found out - equally textbook - it was too late. We were the same age yet he seemed so much older and far more sophisticated. I finished university and landed a job as a marketing assistant in a national American-based franchising company. After saving vigorously for months and months, babysitting around the clock most weekends, I had saved enough money to go, finally, to travel. Just like the brochures had shown. It was my dream in life, all I worked for and all that I focused on since finishing my studies. I had no real desire to live abroad because I loved the safety of my own surroundings too much, but I was definitely consumed by experiences and the need to see the rest of the world. As I planned my next overseas trip I could speak little of anything else and think of nothing further. Researching and researching I planned the trip of a lifetime. My friends would come over and see all the brochures knowing that they needn't ask, I would tell. My two closest friends had been working for longer than me but hadn't yet travelled. After seeing all that was ahead of me, they shyly asked if they too could come along. "The chicks in Paris," I thought. I was thrilled and we went off to our local travel agent to part with our money.

We flew Olympus Air because it was the last remaining smoking airline (and to be fair it was the cheapest). We were astonished that anyone could surrender their fags for that amount of time, especially if they didn't have to. We had no idea what was in store for us. The passengers filled up the aircraft as quickly as the smoke did. No sooner than people had sat down, they had lit up and in an instant the aircraft was filled with smoke, not just cigarette smoke but strong cigar smoke. At first we joined in, enjoying the adultness of it, but pretty quickly the huge discomfort of being stuck in a vacuum full of smoke reticulating through an air-conditioning system for a day and a half became revolting and even us committed smokers couldn't bear it. The flight was jammed with Europeans, mainly Greeks heading home as our flight had an Athens stopover before Paris. We spent the entire flight dozing in and out of cigarette smoke. By the time we touched down in Charles de Gaulle airport we were struggling to breathe and promised each other that if we never saw a cigarette again it would be too soon (that lasted at least twenty-four hours).

Horrified by our appearance and smell upon our entrance into luscious Paris, we hailed a taxi. The driver read the address I had written down on a piece of paper and glancing suspiciously at us through his rear vision mirror started driving. Finally settled, knowing the worst was behind us, our excitement of being in Paris took over and we talked and laughed for the whole drive. We oohed and ahhed at the beautiful streets we were driving along, the statues at the roundabouts, the shopfronts, the gardens, the trees, making notes to visit every one of them, trying to remember where we were and how to get back there. The taxi pulled up at our address and we gasped at the cost. Having no other option but to pay we timidly produced the amount, much to the amusement of our driver. We were still in shock to finally be in Paris, or perhaps in shock at the price of the taxi, but since the accommodation had come at a great rate (my boss had offered us his Parisian apartment on the Avenue Foch, sixth level, number twelve), we accepted the exorbitant taxi fare. The secretary had given me all the necessary information of my boss's Paris apartment, having stayed there herself for her honeymoon. She could hardly contain her disapproval of how someone as low down the chain of command within the company as I was, had been offered the royal palace. She had been overtly unhelpful, giving no travel advice or words of wisdom. She was barely able to explain the finer details of the apartment and its rules. The truth was, my boss had done the same thing when she was my age but had roughed it, and so she leant the apartment out to many.

Ringing the doorbell, an elderly woman called Auroure answered. She was expecting us but greeted us with the same contempt as Carole the secretary back home. Ushering us in through the large iron gates, tutting her disapproval all the way, her stocky build swayed heavily side to side. We passed through a courtyard to a set of steps with a large landing at the top. Beautiful old French doors sat upon the landing, joining each other hand in hand. Handing us the key, she indicated for us to go ahead to floor six, door twelve; information luckily we already knew. With that, she was gone, and we saw very little of her around the grounds over the following four week stay. 'Good riddance,' we muttered to ourselves. Dragging our luggage through the doors, we entered a moderate sized foyer of no real beauty. To the left was a large spiral staircase, very ornate, and we considered the prospect of six floors up. A small timber door sat to the right of the staircase with two buttons. We entered and pushed the 'up' button, leaning back on our bags and awaiting its arrival. After a while and numerous pushings of the button later, we accepted our fate was sealed in the climbing of the staircase and with luggage in hand we began the ascent, comforting each other with the knowledge that the next time we would at least be heading down. We finally reached door twelve, all panting behind us. I pulled the key out and inserted it into the lock, opening the large wooden double doors in front of us. The most amazing parquetry floors greeted us in a foyer filled with sunlight beaming in through the French windows at the far side of the room. The ceilings, incredibly high, allowed the dust particles to dance in the rays of the sun welcoming us in. A magnificent crystal chandelier hung from the ceiling. The effect was mesmerising, crystals sparkling like a room that had just been opened for the first time in centuries. We were three young girls on the other side of the world, freshly independent, standing at the doorway to heaven. Squealing with delight, Addy and Jemma ran through the apartment, amazed at everything it had to offer. Our home for the next four weeks. I didn't squeal, I didn't run, I didn't breathe. I didn't move. I saw my father standing in that foyer, smiling widely, proud and happy. I watched the dust particles intensely, like I was one of them, singing, soaring, weightless, colliding with the world, completely at one with the French air moving in slow motion around me. I would never forget that moment as a pivotal moment in my life. I realised as I stood there that my destiny was not sealed. The hope for possibilities, for the countless dreams dreamt, were bouncing around in that foyer, under that chandelier, hidden behind century old walls with stories I'd never know and people I'd never know. The power seeped into me, to do what I had yet to learn but I was sure, it was going to come back to me, this, this moment, this place in time. A tear dropped from my cheek and I watched it hit the ground. I heard the girls calling for me, yelling at me to stop daydreaming, to come quickly to the master bedroom, the one they had allocated for me, the true goddess of their time in Paris, their best friend ever. The spell drenched me and I touched my cheeks, my shoulders, and looked at my hands. I was new, I was alive, I would live. I ran off in the direction of the girls' voices, keen to be a part of it all.

He was living in the apartment on the ground level in the building opposite ours. I could look down over our balcony and call to him, loud enough so that he could hear. I would do this on many occasions over the ensuing weeks, until finally it was not necessary. Likewise he could yell up to me, echoing through the central courtyard for everyone to hear, then drifting off up into the Parisian sky. I had no idea when we first met that it was his uncle's place, no idea he was on consignment, no idea that he had a wife and a whole life back in St Tropez. All I thought at that beautiful young age was that he was mine, for my Paris life anyway. I can recall the pain, the searing pain even now.

One day, years later I was filling up the petrol in my car at a station and Madonna came blaring out of the garage's speakers. "You abandoned me, love don't live here anymore." I was transported back to Paris and I literally collapsed, the earth exploded beneath me and I sobbed uncontrollably by the side of my car. Someone approached and assisted me up. I remember turning the key in the ignition and nothing else. "Did I pay?" I have often wondered. I can't even recall the petrol station. That song, like so many others, would cause avalanches in my heart and I would be furious at their torment. Now that I'm older I feel the need to embrace it, to almost surrender to it, so scared that it may actually never have happened. Now I can be thankful for the memories and even grateful for my youth, hanging ferociously on to it when deep down I know it's gone.

The night I met him started out innocently enough. It was our third day in Paris and we were waiting out the front of the apartment block for our taxi. He came bounding out through the iron gates with an intoxicating smile in his eyes. He had two friends with him - not that I took much notice - and they were out on the footpath waiting too. He was beautiful, typically French; large brown eyes, almond shaped, high cheekbones and a smile that spread across his entire face. He was wearing a black woollen turtleneck, light coloured denim jeans and expensive looking black leather shoes. His hair was short, dark and scruffy, his skin aglow with a fresh tan, his eyelashes looked fake. The taxi pulled up in front of us and before we could speak he looked at me intently.

"Maybe we should share?" He said, and without a further word he gestured for everyone to get in. His English was perfect, his accent mesmerising. A second taxi arrived, the others jumped in.

"Where are you going?" He asked, sitting close enough to me that I could smell the wool of his shirt.

"St Germain," I managed.

"St Germain it is," he told the taxi driver, and turned to face me. We sat like that the whole way, never once did his eyes leave mine. His friends were chatting away excitedly with mine. We never spoke, didn't move until it came time to pay the driver. We were apart, all of us, very little from that night on.

One night, we kissed out the front of a club. The others had gone in, he had stopped me, holding me back, motioning to his friends that we would only be a minute.

"This club is going to be full with amazing French men wanting to get your attention. It is very popular and very cool. Trust me to look after you, trust me to take care of you in there."

I nodded and, taking hold of his hand, I told him to lead the way into the lions den. He kissed me right there, gently on the mouth, before we made our entrance.

I know Jem is still in touch with Joffrey and his French family, Julien's best friend on that trip, but I made everyone vow after the relationship ended never to mention his name again. They kept their promises even though on numerous occasions I was dying to know, to hear anything about him. Fortunately he had lost touch with Julien - or so he told Jemma.

The month in Paris was unforgettable but the three weeks that followed were engraved into my brain as much as my name was. Work allowed me to take another three weeks off as holiday without pay, my boss understanding the spell of Paris. The girls returned home on the booked flight while I moved in with him, downstairs on the ground level, never bellowing again. The girls were not happy.

"Please don't come home in a box," Jemma said.

"I couldn't bear to tell your family," Addy pleaded.

I assured them I was going to be fine. It was only three more weeks and they both knew him and understood how I couldn't leave him, not yet.

Finally we were alone together, the innocence of three girls away on a carefree holiday gone. We had behaved ourselves around the group and had tried not to let it ruin the girls' time in Paris, but from the moment we had met he was all I could see. We were one. Two bodies meshed, no longer knowing where his limbs stopped and mine started. I no longer cared for Paris, just him. All that had mattered was him, his body on mine. My father had once told me that life was not a spectator sport and finally I understood. I knew it, the moment I stood on that parquetry floor with the sun shining in. It was shining into my soul, opening me up to the possibilities of the angels that would map out my life. I knew the relationship was founded on lust and not love, like all young relationships, but I also knew there was a love of some kind, a strange unique kind, that had stolen my heart and torn it up. It was unlike anything I had felt before. There had never been any signs of another woman, a marriage, someone torn between two lovers and between right and wrong. There were no late night phone calls or early morning dashes for privacy. I admit, I wouldn't have seen it anyway, but I can't recall moments. We were both twenty-two, I wasn't looking for it and I didn't expect him to be any different to me. Not until later anyway, not until it hurt so much I had to relive every moment trying to find the signs.

Paris ended, like most things. He told me to meet him in Singapore in two months' time. He was going there for work for four days. I knew I would go, the pull was so savage. I convinced him I would meet him there, somehow winging it. He whispered to me to make sure I came and I did, with his fingers inside me and his mouth on my nipple. I couldn't bear it and he rolled me over gently to finish himself off inside me.

The truth came six months later. I was packing for our next trip, our next hook up, and an unsent postcard fell out of an old bag I used in Paris.

My darling Estelle, I miss you gravely and
count down the days and nights until we can
be together again. Work is terribly tedious,
however I have picked up something special for
you as an apology for my constant travel, my darling.
I will be back home in St Tropez with you soon.
Your loving husband, Julien.

He cried and told me he was torn, that he loved her and me. I had no idea how to live after that, no idea how to wake up from the suffocating nightmare. I went out night after night, trying to forget. Stupidly I rang him, a female answered, no French accent, someone new. I quit my job and quit my life. I decided to be a spectator after all. Like all first loves, you get over them, but I searched out French men and French women and anything in between just to dull the pain. I still wonder from time to time where he is, why he didn't leave her for me, what he looks like now, if he's still making wonderful love.

Chapter Seven

It was never easy. That's not true, of course in the beginning it was. But there were the milestones along the way. The sun shone brightly like the lamp posts reminiscent of wartime England or the French gaiety associated with romantic walks down the Avenue Foch, but lately I had trouble breathing and I had to breathe or I would stop. I wasn't going back to sleep, I had been tossing and turning already for most of the night. It was time to leave, it had been too long. I tiptoed down the stairs, touching all the familiar surroundings and lightly sweeping up my keys off the kitchen bench. With speed I was behind the wheel, driving fast, the wind searing through the car, through my body and the music so loud it drained out, my brain opening up into nothingness. I enjoyed the pure anonymity of being in the car, in the early hours of the morning with no-one on the roads. It was exhilarating and the chance to have just a moment in time, a small quintessential escape to not be the person I am, was bliss. A love song played on the radio and I cranked it even louder, tears streaming down my face. Why does every song know how I feel but my husband doesn't? Sharply the tune changed to the latest number one hip hop hit in the country, the entrapped soul in me stirred and I wished I could fly, soar, and I sang loudly along with it, tears still streaming. The shrilling tone of my mobile phone on the seat beside me jolted me back into reality, the flashing yellow digits blaring in the darkness. I tried to remember even picking up my phone, considering the speed I left the house in. I took another look at the number coming up on the screen and vaguely recognised it, confused. It felt like a number from the past but one I couldn't quite place. It wasn't an altogether welcoming feeling. The call ended and I neither picked up nor screened it. Thank god. I didn't think I could have dealt with whatever that was.

I wound slowly back home, making my way quietly into the driveway, cutting the engine along the street and killing the radio. I welcomed the silence now, it was enveloping, like the first night home of a new mother who was breastfeeding in the dead of the early hours, alone yet never alone again.

Stepping into the lounge room I heard his warm voice.

"Is that you Sass?"

Something stirred within me, a knowing that the kindest man I'd ever known had spoken my name. As usual I was consumed by a huge surge of guilt and I couldn't work out if it was superficial or serious.

"Hi honey," I mustered up, "yes darling, it's me."

"Are you alright?"

How many times had I consoled myself into being fine. How many times did the average person console themselves into being fine? I wondered, "Should I turn around to my lover, my soul mate and admit, I am not fine? Does he ask to hear the truth or for the rhetoric that marriages fall into?" I thought, "I don't have the courage, I can't push the point, it is late and the threads I have woven into this marriage will not be answered tonight, like the many similar nights before." I started to feel the swell inside me subside.

"Go back to bed honey, I won't be long," I called.

"Did you go out?" He asked me in a sleepy voice, confused.

"No Tom, you must have been dreaming." I felt him retreat to our room.

"Don't stay up all night," he muttered.

Looking out at the night sky I sighed regretfully, wishing there was a reason to stay up all night. I knew I wouldn't sleep but the options were minimal, and the alternatives were few. The morning would bring all the joy of a new day of chores and mindless jobs, so with leaden feet I switched out the lights and travelled in the footsteps of my life partner to our bed, which I knew in my soul would be our bed forever.

The next morning I awoke early, the first one up. I rested in stillness listening to the silence, inviting it to wash over me, careful not to stir Tom. I didn't want my space to evaporate just yet. A lawnmower started up after several failed attempts and instantly my mind had started up and the emptiness vanished. I knew that within seconds the quietness in our house would be filled and not a moment later a child would appear and then another. I still had a chance, organising my children with breakfast, I threw on a pair of sneakers and running shorts, knowing a run would get me out the door. My exit induced tears and tantrums and I quickly shoved the toast in their mouths, with kisses and promises of the park when I returned. It was quiet outside and as I looked back over my shoulder the children were absorbed with Boots & Swiper on the big screen. Free. Once outside I stopped, exhaled, inhaled and breathed. The street was empty. It was 5.30am, but soon it would be a hive of activity. I walked along slowly like I had purpose, but had none. I looked closely at all my neighbours' houses, imagining their lives, wondering if anyone was at all feeling what I was feeling. I looked closely at the details of each of the houses, their paint jobs, gardens, shutters, well-manicured lawns, state of the art sky lights, louvres, bifolds. Shuddering I realised that these things were important to most people. Why not me? Why couldn't I be absorbed with what my house looked like; focused, dedicated. Most of these places were beautiful, worthy of admiration only I just wasn't so admiring. It left a bad taste in my mouth. Up and over the hill I made my way through the small roundabout and up towards the national park. A man walked past me and smiled, a polite morning smile. No teeth, just a grin and a nod. No exchange, thank god, just a suggestion. Relieved, no way near ready to join reality and the beginning of the day, I thought about the man. I knew his type. Mid-fifties, blue and white striped boardies, long baggy and oversized white t-shirt with an exclusive brand plastered across the chest. White baseball cap, mirror sunnies. The greyness of his skin could suggest he smoked and the faint hint of stale beer that followed him possibly indicated that he was slightly hung over, tired and in search of a coffee. Thankfully I encountered no one else as I walked along with my own thoughts. I started humming Elton John's 'Jesse' and before I knew it I'd been swept away with his trailer by the sea. I couldn't recall when or where I heard it but it resonated strongly.

I started to romanticise about the trailer and the sea. The area was rocky, the sand was coarse and the sea way out in the distance was choppy. Sitting there in the middle of nowhere, not a living soul for miles, a sharp cliff jutting out into the ocean, was a rusty old trailer. I saw it as clear as the sky and looked closer at the picture. I watched myself happily reading, a colourful plate of fried eggs, fresh tomato and torn basil on a charming wrought iron verandah setting next to me, an espresso in a small chipped porcelain cup in my hand. I could see myself smiling at something I'd just read then returning the book to the table, finishing the delicious breakfast and looking out into the great expanse of the ocean beyond. There was music playing but I couldn't quite make it out. A car rolled past me and I shook my head at the dream.

Wandering along, I knew I needed a change of scenery. For how long I wasn't sure but long enough to restore and replace the ugliness that was creeping into my soul. The truth was, I had given so much over the last ten years that there was nothing left to give and nothing left to take. Picking up my pace, all sense of wistfulness long gone now that the neighbourhood was fully awake. I quietly hoped that maybe I could head out again tomorrow and pick up where I had left off, as I felt a little more confident about the day of ahead of me than I had earlier.

The plans for the day had already changed by the time I returned home. My son was reading a Harry Potter book and I thought of his invisible cloak, having read the series the year before. I longed for such an item. The thought of that little cracked espresso cup kept popping into my imagination, which made me happy, sadly so if I gave it the thought it required. Trying to organise the morning chaos, I realised nothing further was going to happen until I got some coffee. So throwing the lead on the dog, I bundled up the kids and headed back out to our corner cart where wakefulness awaited me.

When I arrived home later that day it seemed like another world, the escape of the morning a long distant memory. The kids were in the pool laughing loudly, the babysitter keeping vigilant watch. There was the faint sound of music somewhere, only slightly legible over the noise from the whipper-snipper. Trying to stay hidden for a while I absorbed the feeling and let it take over. I loved this family, loved my husband, loved this house that I grew up in and then finally bought off my mother once she decided to move into a city apartment. I loved the sound of water, I always had and I made sure the children understood it too. They had swimming lessons from the age of one and had been taught how to be safe, smart and wise around water. Consequently beach holidays were always the favoured type. I headed down the side of the path towards the noise of the whipper-snipper, waving silently at my husband. He moved the whipper-snipper to one side and I gave him a kiss on the cheek as he allowed me to pass, making my way in through the front of the house so as to surprise the kids at the back. I changed into my swimmers and bomb-dived in to the pool, causing a huge commotion as the kids started screaming frantically. The drenched babysitter left laughing and we continued with antics in the pool.

After a while, jumping out, I lay contentedly at the poolside while the kids played a mermaid and pirate game. The smell of onions cooking woke me and I realised I'd drifted off to sleep. Wondering for how long I slept, I lazily wrapped the towel around me and wandered down to the barbecue area. Casually leaning at the barbecue, Tom had showered and cleaned up and was reading the paper in between turning the onions. He looked up at my arrival and offered a huge grin.

"Hi honey, good nap?"

Nodding I took a sip of his beer, giving him a wink. I picked through the paper, taking out the 'Living' section to peruse the restaurant reviews and any other industry snippets of information. It wasn't long before the smaller ones found us and the newspaper was discarded, ripped away by the children and their activities. Tom quickly grabbed the small glossy insert mag before a glass tipped over and ruined the whole lot, turning it into papier-mache.

"Thanks," I said, "great reflexes."

He returned to the barbecue and the task at hand. The children were given instructions on who was doing what to assist in the delivery of dinner and they ran off to oblige, knowing a treat after dinner would be in store should they do as they were told. I noticed I'd drunk most of Tom's beer and grabbed him another.

"How are you today?" he asked casually. "I noticed you were up and out early this morning."

"Mmm," I responded, pondering the question. "I'm fine. Or I will be fine. You just have to get on with it, right? I mean, I had a pretty restless night last night, but I feel better today."

"What's keeping you up?" he asked, turning to look at me.

"That's the question isn't it? Who knows Tom. It just feels like groundhog day followed by groundhog year. I don't know what I expected, I'm just - I don't know - worried that time is ticking away and I'm making egg sandwiches."

"Honey, it's called life, and I know how much these mundane activities get you down but you just have to suck it up and get over it. There is no point even considering it. One day there will be no egg sandwiches and then you can save the world but for now, it is what it is."

"I know you're right Tom, but it's just not that easy for me to live it. Can't we go away? Aren't we due for a holiday, just an escape for a small time, all of us? I need to stop for a moment, smell something different, not make egg sandwiches."

"Oh Sass. It's impossible, we're so busy at the moment, I've got houses settling all over the place and you're looking to open a new restaurant. Now that you've decided to sell, we can't afford to leave it at the moment. It will slow up soon, and then we can get away for a day or two. Maybe after Christmas, or before the opening of the new place."

I knew the spiel well, and he was right. Only that it doesn't slow down, life never slows down on its own. You have to make it and that's what I was crying out to do, make it! I needed a break. Didn't he know I was starting to flip out more than usual, did I have to spell it out for him? Not that it would do any good, his response would be as he had said: "suck it up, get over it". It wasn't forever, but for me it seemed already like forever. I closed my eyes and shut my mouth, knowing that an argument was all that it would result in. I tried to bring back the image of the trailer. He knew I was unhappy - well not unhappy - but in need of something. But it was Tom's way to discard it, certainly never enter into a discussion about it. Pretend it didn't exist, give it no air play, and it would go away. Reasonably enough too, that is how it had worked for the last ten years. I had complained, cried, nagged, griped and he had not entertained any of it, not yelled, not belittled, not agreed, not anything. He just let me go on, pour out all of my frustration and then did nothing.

It wasn't long before dinner was eaten and baths had been had and the household started to slow down. I found myself back in that place humming Elton John.

My husband and I were married in an amazing event. Fireworks, degustation menu, exquisite wines. We had a quaint marquee on top of the city, the view spectacular and the night unforgettable. He looked at me like every girl wants to be looked at; in awe. And now here we were, a decade later, a couple of children later, a couple of businesses later.

Like every female - and perhaps this is an assumption, but - I woke up, after childbirth had rendered itself finally finished, trying in some small way to regain a body, somehow resembling a younger me but mostly not. I hid any really old photos of myself, reminders not at all welcome at that stage of the process and prayed I could see the merits in the holistic journey I was supposed to be embarking on. There was nothing gratifying about much of motherhood, a good friend declared to me only six months after the birth of her first baby. She didn't mean it awfully just that, all through life up until the time you have children (if you are lucky enough to or decide you wish to), good work is acknowledged if not rewarded. Having a baby is good work, keeping a marriage together after having a baby is even better work, yet still very little acknowledgement and definitely no esteem rewards get pinned to your chest. Of course we know how rewarding motherhood is, how beautiful our children are, how we couldn't live without them and how in love we are with them, but there are still issues to bitch and moan about and for sure we do. I was no different and I was one of the lucky ones. Our first-born and Tom had been inseparable. He sat, crawled, stumbled and walked around behind Tom until there was nothing left to walk behind.

It seemed only natural to procreate again and our daughter was born, the relationship between Tom and her equally special, but between two small children, a restaurant and his business, there was nil alone-time. Tom managed perfectly with no him-time, or so it seemed, and we both managed okay with little us-time, but I struggled with no me-time. It wasn't even like I was tending to children all day; I was working, talking to adults, running our businesses, creating new businesses, dealing with business partners, landlords, solicitors.

I came home from work and Tom was always there, completely supportive, completely encouraging and full of praise for me and the children. It made me want to scream. Our children were healthy, happy and fairly balanced, their dad involved, their parents in love and always happy. But all I could dream of was being far away with a lover, somewhere in the middle of nowhere. I sold businesses, bought businesses, learnt business and lived business. I spoke to my children about money, bank accounts, interest, leases, loans, fair work, policy, famine. Tom read them children's books, coloured in and painted with them, jumped in the sprinkler with them. I did sit ups, exercises and ball skills. It all sounded perfect. We all know opposites attract but what happens when those opposites became too debilitating? What happens when you start to question all of the other options you had before embarking on the pursuit of a lifelong partner? The answer for me changes every time. On a good day there is simply no indulging it, I can't believe my good luck but on a bad day it's so far from where I want to be sitting.

I knew in my soul that whilst my husband and I were worlds apart, fundamentally we were similar. He was mindful, intelligent and receptive and the harmony between us bounced around like a couple on a squash court. I was baffled as to why life wasn't smoother, why our heads had to butt over every single detail. Why did I have to have the last word, and eventually him too? Why did I have to bend and mould or simply shut up to duck the barrage? Why did we both have to win, when there was never a winner?

Chapter Eight

The phone was ringing somewhere and then Tom was speaking. He grabbed his car keys.

"Work," he shrugged at me. "Something is wrong with a contract."

He hugged me, stuffed his phone in his back pocket and I hugged him back. I was half his size, waist to head and I smiled at him as he left. I knew the feeling was unfair and as much as I loved him - and I knew I did, he was my soul mate even if I'm unsure if I believe in such a thing - I was grateful for the alone time. Selfishly I thought again about a holiday and I tried to recall the last one we had. With alarm I realised it was almost five years ago. We had all gone to a gorgeous little island, accessible only by boat, for ten days. The island was remote and elegantly understated. We packed daily culinary feasts and imported expensive wines. Bikes, scooters, balls - everything was included. The anxiety however at being on a remote island, so far removed from work, took a little to get used to, and by the time we had actually unwound enough to enjoy the holiday it was over.

After that, Tom decided that for the time being quick and close holidays were the only way to travel.

The children one by one started to fall asleep until all there was left was the sound of various television shows and DVDs playing in each room. Carefully I went around and closed down the audio devices and dimmed all the lights. Picking up the remote I was hopeful that there was a mindless movie screening, one I could zone out from and indulge in a bucket of ice cream with. Perfect - a Hollywood cliché with a couple of big star names was starting in ten minutes. I grabbed one of the kids' doonas that had fallen to the floor from a tussle earlier and cocooned myself in it, set for a night of bliss.

It was later, after I received the text, that I racked my brain for the name of the movie. It was of no consequence but even years later it annoyed me that I couldn't remember.

The text came two minutes later, "I've been arrested." With a full stop. "I'm on my way to jail." Another text, another full stop. My husband, who only an hour ago was bathing my children. I tried to stay calm, talking to myself in quiet tones. I thought of Tom, this patient, kind and caring man, father-of-the-year sort of material. Jail? It was so foreign to the man I knew, the man who just left. I blinked and tried to steady myself on the back of the couch, reading the message again, imploring it to say something else, hopeful even for a simple explanation. Nothing came. Just yellow words staring at me from a black screen. They penetrated me, stretched over my entire being. What could possibly have gone wrong? What had provoked this, who had provoked this? I turned to anger. Anger at the thought of the children, the worst possible scenario passing through my brain. With that I started to panic. Then myself. God forbid how I was going to do any of this without him. He held this unit together; our rock. Before the layers started to peel away and the wheels started to fall off I texted back. "Are you ok?" I waited. Nothing. Five more minutes. Nothing. I assumed it was all too late, having no idea what was too late. Maybe the interrogation had begun, he was no longer contactable and the worst had arrived at our doorstep. I was completely underprepared and completely out of control. I was ringing now, frantic. No answer. I rang again, furiously this time, so fast that I'd ended the call before it had begun. I tried again, slower. Still nothing. I tried his work number, angry that I hadn't thought of it sooner. It rang, he answered.

"Hello, how did you go?"

"Tom, oh my god, are you okay?" Later I recalled the pause; I heard it straight away at the time.

"Sass?" Almost a question, maybe surprise, maybe concern.

"Of course," I said. "Who were you expecting?" Without waiting for an answer I barged on. "What is going on Tom?"

He stumbled. "I'm not sure," he said. "What do you mean, is everything okay?"

Now totally confused, I told him about his text. About his being arrested and going to jail.

"Hello? Was that you or am I losing it?"

"Oh shit honey," he said, "I didn't mean to scare you. It's nothing, I'll have it sorted by the morning, it was unpaid parking fines. It's a misunderstanding really, I'm back in the office now. I shouldn't have worried you."

Completely baffled, I tried to digest the situation. He told me he would ring me in an hour when he knew more and hung up. A pit formed low in my stomach and I noticed the phone was shaking in my hand. Taking a deep breath, I put the phone down, away from my line of sight, and walked slowly towards the children's room, needing them like I had never needed them before.

Having fallen asleep in one of the kids' beds, I slowly attempted to remove myself from the entanglement without disturbing their sleep. As I quietly made my way down the hall towards our room I saw Tom's wallet. He was home safe and sound after all. Tired and pissed off with the whole ordeal, I decided to let the argument wait for the morning. Walking up to the bedroom I could hear him before I saw him, his breath rising and falling in its rhythmic way. He was in bed fast asleep and tiptoeing around the room I realised I was holding my breath, so afraid to wake him. I didn't want this to wait until the morning, I didn't want to have this at all. I prayed that when I woke up it would be a new day. The text I received and, more importantly, the phone call I had with him, did not add up. Lightly lying in bed and holding my frame up, not wanting to disturb even the air around me, I dozed off to sleep.

The next morning presented torrential rains, coming down fast and furious. I opened the curtains to our balcony somewhat gingerly, the rain looking even more serious from where I stood, like a solid wall rather than a solid sky. I returned to bed, lying wide awake and listening to the sound of the rain on our bedroom roof. I quietly turned to Tom. Confused, I stretched out my arm, my palm resting firmly on the mass next to me. Pulling away what seemed like dozens of pillows and cushions I saw that his side lay empty. Wide awake now, jumping up like the clown in the children's windup box, I bound down the stairs in the direction of the cartoons playing on the TV. Surely he had not left already? There were things that need discussing. The children were sitting calmly, watching their favourite show and one of them looked up at me as I appeared. With a forced casualty I asked:

"Where's Dad honey? Good morning."

"He left already mummy," he replied. "To pick up some things for work."

"Mummy," they asked, "can we have tuckshop today?"

Struggling to hear them over the rain bearing down on the verandahs and the swirling going through my head, I tried to stand still. I was interrupted by a tugging at my shirt. Looking down, my youngest was staring up at me.

"Mummy, can I have a chocolate sandwich, and can you tell Monty to put Dora on?"

I looked at her angelic face and crouched down to give her a hug. On autopilot the Nutella was found, the sandwich was made and Dora was switched over. This started the opinion polls on why Dora gets priority and why not Dance Studio or Prank Patrol? And just like that, a switch flicked and all the noise around me started to fade, getting

48

fainter and fainter and further away until it felt like a vacuum of muted silence had taken me hostage. A strange sensation overcame me. I could probably make out the words my children were hurtling at me but my concentration slid. Everything went into slow motion, there was no interest in the movements around me. I wondered if I had snapped, changed sides, finally left the mind of the sane and crossed over into psychosis. And if so I was surprised, but questionably not at all unhappy. It felt liberating. I saw myself swimming though cool calm waters. A canal, with houses lining the riverbanks. Empty, motionless. Small splashes of water fell from swaying trees. I could feel the warmth of sun on my face. The trees above all but gone. Lifting my chin I let it soak through my skin down through my bones. Was this heaven? I took notice of the houses as I floated along the river, lying on my back, enriched by the sun. I watched the flickers of light through the tree's branches and the silent birds having a tea party above the leaves. I could feel my limbs, my heart, my eyes, grow strong. I reached the end of canal, giant-like, lying between the banks, my toes touching the mouth of the river and my elbows resting on the houses rooves. It was like a bath with my oversized head leaning against a sandbank, watching tiny boats and ships going along the broadwater. I was naked and the sun was covering every skin cell. No one paid attention to me. The tiny figurines and lives dotted around me were getting on with things. I was an island. normal, something that had been there forever. Not mysterious or unusual. Just there, like always. A large land mass, why should that cause a stir?

There was a beacon flashing in the distance, it made me lethargic. I closed my eyes in the vast body of space where I had consumed all the oxygen. Up ahead I felt a shadow coming in my direction. A tear dropped, sad to lose the sunlight. The flashing beacon returned, I could see it through the layers of my eyelids. I should turn back. The beacon was starting to fade, now behind me, in the distance. Had I gone too far? Would I know my way back? I should remove my heavy limbs from the shadow, or my bones would start to melt, morph into the night-time that was on its way, just waiting, patiently. Would there be a familiar route back or would I have to try something new? My fingers crawled slowly across the land, out of the canal, away from the broadwater. They dug into the earth and dragged me along, knowingly, still strong from the heat. I came up for air and slid back down to size in order to fit between the rows of houses. I took a look around, chose a direction to head in.

With my first gulp of air Dora screamed at me loudly through the TV. A stranger was staring at me through my glass door out on my verandah under the pouring rain outside. He had a policeman's uniform on. He was young. He was knocking on the oversized glass doors, holding an umbrella, completely dry. Through the rain I noticed a second man, he also had a policeman's uniform on and was standing down on the path, away from the verandah, that led from the front of the property to the back. I wondered if there was a stream of them lining up, single file to my front gate, like ghosts or tin soldiers. There was still a knocking on the door. Wearily, like logs being pulled from a riverbank, I took a step towards him, acknowledging him. I turned back around, for one last look at what I was about to lose, what I was about to never regain and reached out towards the door. My children were silent as I turned the handle. I looked at their faces; wide-eyed, mouths open. Briefly I considered their little minds, their unknowing thoughts, then disregarded it, pointless for it bore no help. In that moment I turned into a different woman and with complete composure I opened the large sliding door.

"Yes officer, please come inside out of the rain."

He said my name, "Sassy Birmingham," more of a confirmation than a question.

"Yes," I agreed.

He proceeded with details and facts, a story that changed someone's life. He continued quickly, trying to get it over with it, spewing information. Curiously I watched him, this young man with this overwhelming responsibility, here to advise me - someone he had never met and knew nothing about - that he had bad news. He continued, he continued, he continued. Quietly in myself, I snapped. The calmness that had entered me had fled, replaced with a dripping of lead-like dread, dropping rhythmically on my head, bang, bang, bang. My spine started to sink into the ground, like a nail under the blast of a hammer, my hips, my waist followed, inevitable. Hot lava oozed from my eyes, a slowly simmering volcano. It rolled silently down my cheeks and I looked down at the timber floorboards to where my feet had vanished; I was neck deep already. To look at this man's face, I couldn't bear it. Was he to become my last memory? Was he to be the one thing I remembered most for the rest of my life? I couldn't have him at the end, I thought hysterically, I couldn't have him at the end! He would leave, go back to his wife, girlfriend, mother, father, dog, cat, house, street, his life, he would describe to someone my grief, his awkwardness, my reaction. He would feel sad, he would pity the children. Someone would comfort him, someone would be there for him, he would get dressed again and go on again. I couldn't let him be included, I couldn't have him in my life. I didn't even know his name and yet he would always be there. The tears were falling now, rapidly into the quicksand around me, he was saying my name too many times, it was ringing, it was too many times. That many times was unnecessary, even I knew that. He had more to tell me and finally he told me again, it was an accident, nobody's fault, there was nothing anyone could do. My eyes stared through him. He gave me his card, said I was needed to identify him. He asked if he should call someone. I wondered who the fuck he thought he should call. God, fate, time, the wheel of fortune? I shook my head. He left with his sidekick who finally moved off his spot on my path. I turned to the children.

"What did he want?" I heard.

"Nothing," I lied. "They were checking on the neighbour's dog, apparently he is lost. Who wants some ice cream?"

I loaded them in the car, fixated on getting ice cream. We drove directly towards the twenty-four-hour 7/11. Once inside I bought a bucket of ice cream, cones, topping and hundreds and thousands. I went back to the car. I used my fingers to dig out the ice-cream and moulded it in to each one of the cones, pouring the syrup over the top and tipping the sprinkles on to finish. The kids lunged for them, delighted at the mess and frivolity. Before they had even started I asked who wanted seconds and began the process. They discarded the first ice-creams, dropping them to the floor as I handed them their next. The two year old threw up arnd I uselessly cleaned her with some items of clothing off the car floor. Sitting back in my seat I vomited too, dry-retching and convulsing.

I started the car and began to drive, my hands gripping the wheel, covered in vomit. After some time I pulled over in a quiet street. The rain had stopped and the sun was somewhere in the distance. The kids were asleep in the back, bits of ice cream stuck to them and I was still covered in vomit. I couldn't release my hands from the wheel. My head slumped over, lying heavily on my hands. The despair was overwhelming. I made no noise. I tried not to but I thought of the children in the back and had trouble breathing; I couldn't remember how to do it. I felt myself going blue, gagging. Shaking my head I made myself sit up and, quickly opening the door, I threw up again. I couldn't leave them as well, even though I already had.

My in-laws said they would take the kids for a couple of weeks to give me some time. I could let my defences down, heal. I took any instructions, was told what to do. My mother was out of her depth and had no idea how to help or what to say. She tried for a while then stayed away, leaving care parcels for me and the children on the front verandah. It was strangely comforting. The great sadness and loss consumed me and the unanswered questions were out in space somewhere, no doubt waiting to surface within me. The children came home early, we needed each other too much. They were my recovering, my healing, the only reason to turn over in the morning, to breathe. That split second when you wake up and don't remember.

Months later, an officer appeared at my house with a box. Remains of luggage from the boot of Tom's car found near the accident. Without looking, I suddenly realised. He had been leaving and then he died.

Chapter Nine

He had not meant for it to happen. Couldn't even recall the finer details. The thing was and it wasn't. It wasn't anything unusual to begin with and, as it happened, nor to end with either. The strength of the economy had created a series of ebbs and flows and had resulted ultimately in a huge success in his business. People were still buying, and houses were still selling and in his area, particularly. Sure the hours were long, but whose weren't, and he was killing it. He had always been a businessman, had a knack at making a buck. There was no denying his natural intelligence, a gift he was born with, never having to work too hard at school or university. His good looks and honest approach put him way ahead of others. He was a kind and caring man in the main but if you crossed him, you would know. He learnt early on in life the value of listening, instead of occupying. He listened intently when someone spoke to him, sometimes with interest but most times not. He started a conversation with a question and bingo, the floodgates opened. His intelligence and depth of general knowledge allowed the conversation to flow and if it suited him he could engage for hours and hours. He cared little for idle chit-chat but knew it was necessary. He despised gossips and boredom. He was well liked and harboured no ill will towards anyone. He could live with or without people apart from the special few. He had three true friends; work, family and children.

He did however love his wife, helplessly. I was like no one he had ever met before. This is how he saw me: the moment I spoke he knew I was different, knew I had something that was missing in most people. He had been captivated and intrigued. He realised which had surprised and excited him; this was normally his field of expertise, he was the engager and yet I had him talking, telling me things he had told no one. In return I gave him nothing. I was aloof, somewhat guarded but charming and encouraging. He had felt totally at ease with me, comfortable and strangely safe, a feeling he was quite unaccustomed to. I had a natural confidence that was rare, a confidence that was so subtle it overpowered him. He knew he would never tire of me, I was unique and captivating. I was real and he trusted that, knowing it would save his life.

It wasn't easy though, I had men at my feet, happy just to be there. When I smiled the whole room stopped and looked, my laugh was toxic, rare and genuine. It was a laugh that echoed in my eyes, compelling others to laugh alongside me. My long eyelashes stood bright above my wide eyes and my slender physique highlighted my brightness. My slightly square cheekbones and olive skin were inherited from my father and when I lifted my eyes to smile at someone, they wanted me to never look away. My lips were large and full, standing out against my lean frame. My hair was always slightly messy. He had persevered, I was all he could think of, nothing else mattered. We were twenty-six and had the world at our feet, he knew together we would work. He bet his four closest friends he would marry me and two years later he did. It was the happiest day of his life. I was intoxicating and he couldn't get enough of me.

Even as he drove away that early morning, almost fifteen years later, his heart was breaking. With every mile he drove it hurt more and more. He had no idea why I was so unhappy. He knew I left late in the night and returned home early in the morning, he knew I roamed the streets early in the morning, late at night, sad. His mind was going crazy, he had no idea how to help me, or if in fact he could. I was still all that mattered to him. He bought the house at the beach in the hope that it was where we could reunite, reconnect, go back to the magic that had been with us for so long. He knew at his core, just like he did the moment we met, that he couldn't be without me. The house was supposed to be a surprise. We had talked of it all our lives. I wanted holidays and time out and this was going to be the answer. After that, the place in France that we had dreamed of too was bought, another ten years later. He got the key the night before, would have had it earlier if the police hadn't pulled him over for unpaid traffic offenses and threatened to lock him up. Luckily he managed to get hold of his mate in their head office and convince the officer that he was not a flight threat and paid the outrageous bill. The real estate agent finally tracked him down back at the office, but by then it was too late to head south so there he was, trying to have it ready for me by that night, leaving early in the morning so he didn't have to face the thousands of questions he knew I would ask.

He didn't see the truck coming. He had picked up a hitch-hiker after a quick dip at the beach. He needed a lift into town and it was on his way, the guy had nothing, not a bag, not a coat. He had only just started the engine and merged into the highway when the truck hit. All his thoughts were on me, my surprise, my happiness, my joy and then there was nothing. I was gone, Sass was gone.

Chapter Ten

"A Broken Heart is Blind" is singing from the speakers as I enter the bar. It was close to closing time and I wasn't sure if it was too late for a nightcap.

"Of course not," the boys behind the bar echoed, handing me a wine list.

I wandered over to the corner where a lonely bar stool stood and settled myself in. There were only a few others milling around, maybe six at the most, and my wine appeared on cue. The proprietor was entertaining his mates at the bar, no doubt the reason for the exodus of the last remaining patrons. The boys started to turn it up a notch when the door finally shut. The music was amplified and the cheap cream-coloured curtains were drawn across the windows on either side of the entrance. The American Express sign hanging from the front door was flipped over, informing anyone interested that the bar was closed. There was still some passing traffic and they looked in mainly to investigate the source of the loud music escaping from the closed glass door. They quickly kept moving when they saw the group at the bar too familiar to be guests. A barman walked past me.

"Do you want me to leave honey?" I asked. "I realise you've closed."

He shook his head. "Nup you're fine, if you don't mind them," he nodded in the direction of the gathering at the bar, "they certainly won't mind you. We've got another couple of hours yet before we'll be done."

He moved on, leaving me feeling very honoured to be allowed to occupy some of their intimacy. The longer I lingered here the longer I found it hard to leave. There was an atmosphere of safety tucked behind the curtains, the lights low, the room small, the music loud. I thought about the mess I was in. I knew I was running away, trying to shut it out, but my head wouldn't stop spinning. Where was he going? Who was he going to? The children and I had at least started to piece back our life together and then this. A fucking policeman telling me he had fucking luggage in his boot. I couldn't even ask a question of him, that officer just stood there with the three bags and said:

"We overlooked the luggage at the time of your husband's accident. These were in the boot."

The only part of the car intact. He left them there, three bags of my husband's most treasured possessions, dumped at my doorway all neat and tidy, just like his departure. I took the final sip of my wine, looking for a distraction. "I can do this at home," I reprimanded myself. I turned and looked at the group at the bar behind me, feeling them, trying to soak up their mood. They seemed carefree, if only for the time right now. I loved being hidden here, tucked away from reality and knowing eyes. The music hit an all-time high and the Black Keys pumped out into the room once more … a broken heart is blind... The boys were now singing along with reckless abandonment in reckless pitch. Their drunken passion for the artist and his crooning was loud and the waiter signalled to me for another. I pointed at my watch, "Enough time?" He nodded in the direction of my empty glass and I smiled and shrugged, why not? No one was paying attention to me and I was overwhelmed with gratefulness. I put my money down when the drink arrived, assuring him it was my last. The owner came over to apologise for the level of the music and gave me my money back.

"Not a chance," I said, "it has been perfect. I'll finish the wine and leave you all to it, looks like you're in for a long night."

He laughed and said, "It's my mate's head-wetting, he's just had his first child so we're all pretty chuffed. He's been trying for some time, it's a small miracle."

There was a lull between songs and the boys were robust in their conversation. The topic: at what age did the lead guitarist of this song first have sex. It was discussed with drunken authority and conviction, intimate knowledge by all, the age was swirled around and around. They all drunkenly agreed on twelve. I smirked, twelve! Men!

One of them announced, "Let's get fucked up tonight!" before the next song exploded from the speakers, bouncing off the walls.

Lines of coke were meticulously being cut at the bar and the lights dimmed even further. Tomorrow would hurt. I reached out for my wine glass and collided with the owner depositing a line on the bench in front of me. He said nothing and walked away. It was a lock in and apparently I was in the lockdown. Not wanting to insult anyone and with a great rush of need I accept the gift like someone had just thrown me a lifeline. The tone of the music changed and so did my mood. A sombre ballad sprawled forth and the boys moved from a frenetic energy to a wallowing sadness. There was no joy in this and definitely not what I needed, so I snorted the line and headed over to the iPod. The boys were so consumed with their musical torture, not even noticing me spin the wheel back on the iPod to the abrasive music first played. I returned happily to my seat and tapped along, forgetting myself. The song ended and so did the moment. Considering the babysitter, I threw down a fifty on the table, knowing it should be a lot more, and exited through the stage door.

Wandering home I knew there was a bomb ticking quietly away and I tried to forget the countdown. Luckily everyone was forgiving and accepting when you were in mourning, so the two A.M finish high as a kite would be ignored.

Chapter Eleven

Why did stepping onto a train for a two-hour journey seem so eerie? I was a woman who travelled to far and exotic places, succeeded in business and was capable of making many decisions on any one day – why did I feel this anxious? It was a beautiful summer's day, the sun was streaming in through the windows and I took a seat somewhere isolated, remote. There were very few people aboard so my options were many. I finally decided on a seat, sat down and fished through my handbag to check that I had everything, still feeling a little apprehensive about taking the train and in fact trying to understand why I was, when my car was working perfectly well at home in the garage. I was acutely aware that this was for Tom, trying to come to some understanding of what my head was thinking. Checking all the contents of my bag I started to panic, furiously searching for my phone and noticing instantly it wasn't there. I tried to retrace my steps, remembering the last time I used it was at home - luckily not in the taxi that drove me to the station. "It must be there," I reassured myself, trying to calm the rising terror. One would think I was going to Istanbul or Pakistan in the middle of a coup, an uprising. No one would imagine I was merely heading north to my sister's place at her idyllic beachside home. Not for the first time today I gave myself another talking to. It was getting ridiculous how complicated I was becoming. I knew I looked the part, I was skilled at portraying the perfect image; camel wedges, strapless sun dress, lace bolero, large purple earrings, my hair long and tousled with strands of blonde and brown ribbons. I was still wearing all my wedding jewellery. Tiffany engagement ring and diamond encrusted wedding band, oversized sunnies. I had my book and my journey and to others looked like I had not a care in the world. I hoped, for some unknown reason, people presumed I was childless. I sometimes liked the idea and had the intent to surprise, probably more to shock. On reflection, I didn't really care what these strangers on the train thought. I would survive, the children were being looked after. My only real concern. As I passed through various stations the train started to fill. A woman behind me was reading some inane children's chapter book to her two children and I hoped they would be gone before the long stretch ahead of me. A lady opposite me had luggage, serious luggage. Wherever she was going she was going for some time. She was composed, nicely presented, had good skin. Her phone rang, she answered in a voice I knew all too well. Sad, croaky, defeated.

"I'm not coping all that well," she said into the phone. "Has Frasier arrived?"

The rest of the conversation was drowned out by the womans voice behind me getting louder and louder as she continued reading to her children. It was peculiar, I thought, for a mother to be such an exhibitionist. The majority of the carriage was now being read to. To everyone's great relief she eventually alighted, but not before declaring "The end" which someone replied "Thank god" to. My sister was expecting me to call, to let her know I was on the way but with the absence of my phone that hadn't happened. Hopefully she would rely on my late night phone call and meet me anyway. It was a spur of the moment thing. She was complaining about her consuming life as a mother. Having just had her second baby and with her husband constantly working, she was travelling the 'single mother with a baby' route and getting pretty fed up. Being way up on the coast also meant she had no family and her main support network was obviously other mothers in the same situation. It was all getting a bit too claustrophobic. She was sick of talking about children. I on the other hand had buried myself in mine since the funeral. I spent every waking moment checking on them, terrified something would happen to them too. At school I would wait until at least half an hour after the bell rang before I could leave, watching them through the classroom window until a teacher or parent volunteer noticed me and gave me that look of pity, of vague understanding. At some point the teacher met with me to gently let me know that the kids were doing ok.

"They obviously don't understand the full impact of the situation, but who does?" she said.

They were interacting fine, just like four-year-olds should be, and participating exceptionally well given the circumstances.

"You should be proud of them, you have both clearly done a great job raising them."

I wanted to scream at her, "They're four! We haven't raised anything yet and we will not be raising anything ever again!"

Everyone told me children were resilient, mine were young. I nodded and agreed, thanking them for their opinion, which meant absolutely nothing to me. I knew the impact on them would be huge; now, sooner, later, forever. What a myth, that children were resilient. What was it supposed to mean anyway? They wouldn't harm themselves at bad news? Take their lives? Take someone else's life? Did that mean they were resilient? Because they didn't know what their options were, yet? One day they would, and these so-called 'resilient children' would be found out to be not so resilient. Maybe a good look at the juvenile delinquent centres or the youth crime rates would be a good indication. Maybe more thought, more theories, more research into children not being resilient would be more beneficial in the long run.

We stopped in the middle of nowhere. The station was buzzing, there were people everywhere. In my carriage there was great activity, people hopping on and off by the droves. It reminded me romantically of the famous Gare de Lyon only nothing at all like it. I looked for beauty on board and not surprisingly was disappointed. In this part of the world beauty existed only in the eye of the beholder. The lady across from me started to weep uncontrollably in absolute silence. She was sitting on a double bay suitcase on the seat next to me. I was forced to look away, feeling the tears in my eyes spring into action. I realised I didn't know her sadness, her deep pain, but it was there and it would, like mine, define her forever. I knew I couldn't imagine her story or her situation but I was too exhausted and if I was to be honest, too afraid of where I might end up. Whatever the circumstances, there was nothing surer than that her life would change course permanently. Sadly, time doesn't allow us to go back. 'Time is always on your side' - the cliché. But what if I didn't get the time, what if I lost, if I didn't make it that far? Time had become my enemy. It was not moving fast enough, I wished it away from the moment I woke up. I wanted it to speed through me like the express rail I was on, propelling me into the far future, where all of the hard work had already been done, behind you.

Two teenaged boys started singing, they were good and the train started to relax. People began to enjoy the lightness of the boys' young voices and the innocence they implied. They couldn't be more than sixteen years old yet they sat together, both side by side, looking out the window and singing harmoniously in unison. Sandy blonde floppy hair and short military-style dark brown hair. One day they might be part of a boy band or simply a duo, famous, and I'd see them being interviewed or would watch snippets of their live concert being reported on at prime time news hour and I'd remember them now, lulling the occupants of the carriage into a smooth rhythmic trance as the train pushed sluggishly forward.

A young lady was facing me. Earphones were in her ears, she had large black round sunnies, curly brown hair tied back in a loose ponytail, and a round face. She was smirking away, oblivious to the singing and the crying girl. She smiled to herself like she knew the biggest secret in the world, like the cat that caught the mouse. I wanted to stare her out of her smugness but the darkness of her glasses hid the movement of her pupils. I wanted to show her the face of loss, push the lady across from me into her face, make her understand how everyone is hurting - even the boys singing. I couldn't remove her from my vision and she had my heart pulsing. There was no other word than smug, it was genuinely infuriating. I looked through my handbag to try to distract myself from this lady who was now laughing quite loudly at a text she was reading. I got up and moved; I was close to hitting her. As we neared our destination, coming out of remoteness and plunging into a tourist mecca, the people noticeably started to change alongside the scenery. Gone were the casual, untidy, simple folk. Now the train filled up with perfume, the sound of bangles clanging, laughter, mobile phones, warmth. These people brought warmth. It was not the brown uncovered skin everywhere, the knowledge that Festivale was around the corner with its bright parties and colourful attire; it was the attitude, the happiness, the confidence. It was what I needed and I straightened up, trying to look the part.

I applied my gloss and pretended. I put up my façade and relied heavily on my rising sign, the one that presents oneself to the outside world as a reflection of what I wanted them to see. An image of the collection of personalities I had gathered over the years, the best one being put forth. Unexpectedly, a great emotion of sadness overcame me and I couldn't deny any longer how much I missed him. I wished fervently that he was here, beside me, his handsome face smiling right through me, knowing how much I would be loving this change of atmosphere, gaiety abounding. I missed his strong athletic body, his grey eyes, his need for me to need him. I took a deep breath and attempted to regain myself, check myself, pull it together and prepare for my stop and my departure. A great surge of people headed towards the doors as the train pulled in and slowly came to a grinding halt.

At the station I walked tall and proud, confident like everyone else around me. Only my hands were rubbing together in anxiety, my rings twirling around my fingers giving me away. I went to take them off and follow through the facade, reinvent myself for today, for tonight. Maybe it was the way forward, who knew with these things? The attempt was feeble and I couldn't pull it off - or them off for that matter. Instead I achieved the complete opposite, gripping them tightly, utterly terrified of this new world I had entered. Tears stung my eyes, my hands were folded over one another in a gesture that appeared united but they were arguing continually. I found my past and held on to it tightly; not at all what I had intended.

Striding through the crowd looking for my sister, searching the approaching faces I finally saw her waving madly. Tears streamed down my face at the sight of her, this person who loved me so unconditionally for all of our lives. I grabbed onto her, both of us unable to speak, unmovable under the weight in our hearts.

Later that night I told her about the luggage, the strange phone call the night before he left, and died. I hadn't told anyone about the luggage and the confession brought relief.

"It just doesn't make sense," she said.

"I know," I agreed, "I can't work it out. I've spoken subtly with everyone who knew him but no one has said anything," I say, confused.

When they arrived in droves after his funeral month after month to help and offer support, I had cautiously quizzed. This was before I had even known his car was full of luggage. No one provided anything. No one knew of any arrest, of trouble, of going to jail, of something wrong, some sort of danger he might have been in, a mess, a reason to leave town.

"Maybe they knew but didn't want to say," she went on. "Who would want to divulge that sort of information to a grieving wife?"

"I would!" I replied, mortified. "Who wouldn't want to help a grieving wife with the grief? It's ludicrous!"

"Sass, maybe it's more than you could bear. Maybe it's just better that you don't know. Have you ever thought of that?" she asked.

"Do you know something Brig? Is there something you thing you need, to tell me" I asked, so fearful I realised I was holding my breath.

"Of course not, Sass! Please tell me, you know I would tell you anything. I can see the pain you're in. I couldn't sit here and lie to you. I also can't sit here and even imagine there was a problem in the first place. He loved you Sass, he was so wrapped up in you. You have to know that at the very least there would definitely have been no one else. That is just not Tom," she told me adamantly, her eyes staring directly into mine. "He wasn't a man with close friends. Whatever secret he had been keeping or whatever trouble he was in he would no doubt have told no one."

"I think you're right. He was such a vault. If there was something I don't think he would have told anyone anyway. He would never have wanted to burden anyone. I don't know what's worse? I'm so scared of what could have been, it's hard for me to move on. I keep thinking 'it's not over', I keep holding my breath, waiting for the moment when I'm going to fall down even further. It's awful, it's so awful."

She produced theory after theory, all harmless, trying to pacify me and keep me calm. We stayed up through the night talking, crying, staring. She brought me tea, warm milk, tissues, foot balm. I couldn't stop talking, for hours I told her all my fears for the future, for the children. She comforted me as I knew she would, assuring me, her and Tom's family would look after all of us forever. I knew she was right, knew the children loved his parents, his brothers and sisters and their families. I knew I would not be forgotten, they would not be forgotten and they were hurting too. But what of me? What of me without him? I couldn't imagine this new life I had. I looked for him everywhere. I called his name, honestly expecting an answer. I told my sister that only yesterday I actually called out to him angrily for not responding.

"You can't think like that anymore," she said calmly. "The children, the restaurant - that's what needs you now, focus on them. Time is a healer, accept he is gone in your own time but begin to accept it, for the sake of the children if nothing else." She carried on, "Why don't you organise a trip? Not for right now but for later, after, when you're up to it. Book it now for a year's time. See where you're at when it comes around. I read this was a healing technique."

"A trip? It's the last thing on my mind. The train ride was hard enough Brig." I was trying not to cry.

"Not for now," she said softly. "For later. You may need it later Sass. Please say you'll do it?" she said firmly.

"I'll think about it Brig. Where would I go?" I asked.

"To the beach of course, to the beach," she said.

Chapter Twelve

There were many things I couldn't do. Painting, drawing, giving a compliment, receiving one. Poetry, drawing straight lines, cleaning, washing clothes separately, looking after animals, tennis, any kind of water sports, flossing, tolerating fools. And there were many things I hadn't done. Meditated, sky dived, smoked pot, triathlons, acting, a threesome, raised money for charity, eaten eel, backpacked. It wasn't so much of a bucket list, I was well aware but pointing out some of the obvious. Brig had gotten me thinking. Maybe a trip was not such a bad idea. I definitely had no intention of eating eel but that didn't mean I couldn't attempt some of the other things. Ok, probably not raising money for charity either - I was no good at attention to detail, particularly other people's details; that was Tom's thing.

It had been a year since he died, since Brig and I had had the conversation about planning a trip. I booked New Caledonia just to make her happy. I had no intention of going but the thought of it had helped at times over the past year. I gave it adequate thought, had weighed up the alternatives and decided I would go and backpack not only to New Caledonia but to other places as well. Some meditation and peace was what I was craving now. The material on backpacking was huge. Best locations, hot at the moment, "Don't look back, backpacking for life". I realised that people genuinely lived like this, year after year as a permanent lifestyle. I couldn't imagine calling an oversized duffle bag my home for my whole life. "Hold on, please come over, bring a plate, we'll be dining by the side of the road. You can't miss it, it's the large maroon sleeping bag with horizontal black stripes. How's seven?" Some of the photos I saw were of elderly couples camping in the middle of nowhere special. Some bushland depicting anywhere. Maybe if it was the Sahara Desert or the great dunes of Egypt, but camping just in the middle of some crusty uninspiring twigs was beyond me. One couple, Jan and Allen, had their album posted on their backpacking website. There were photos of them as young adults in much the same surrounds. I wondered if they actually just lived on acreage, never once having left, and this was their façade. Even a couple of ocean shots over the years wouldn't go astray. I was hoping for bonfires, killer waves, Coronas, tattoos. Remote untouched scenery only foiled by a spattering of humans squatting in various trees. Should I have considered going with a girlfriend or my sister? I decided against it; this was my list and not anyone else's and anyway, maybe there would be more. The kids were amused by my backpack training and eagerness, secretly believing it would all be over in the first weekend and I'd be booked into a hotel calling for fresh outfits.

Secretly I had wondered too, yet here I was, not having bathed in a week, brushing my teeth with a water bottle, wearing my knickers inside out and tying my hair up with pieces of my hair it was that dirty. What a ball. The children safe at home with Poppy and Nan, I had become envious of those old couples I saw on the websites who actually did this for a living, month after month, year after year.

The town where I stayed was surreal. It was backpacker heaven as the brochures promised, but it omitted some of the warning labels: size two only, no white or pale skin, females must have long hair - the sun-kissed type, males must be equally good looking. It was a playground to the rich and famous bored kids, who had decided to piss their parents off by getting some ink and body piercing. Ordering a coffee from the friendly waiter who had just arrived at my side, I slunk down into a chair, trying to hide amongst the beauties. I picked up an old magazine lying on the table next to me and flicked through it.

"Obesity Epidemic in Texas" read the frontline. Apparently walking was a huge issue in Texas. The average American walks about 1k a day when in Texas it was 20 metres. The article went on to describe how a lady drove her son down to the bus stop at the end of their street even though it was close enough that she could see if from her kitchen window. She told the interviewer that she had never contemplated her son walking there 'when she had two perfectly good cars!". Another man said he collected his mail when driving in or out of the garage, as he had never walked up or down his driveway since he moved there twenty years ago. Looking around, I thought maybe some of those heifers should come here, it might make the place seem a little more normal. Even the waiter who brought me my coffee was a pin up for Ripcurl.

A lady took a seat beside me and the tables were so close I couldn't help but look. Smiling I said, "Hi, what a beautiful place to visit."

She turned to look at me and I caught my breath quickly at how beautiful she was.

"Yes, and it's an even more beautiful place to live. Annika," she said, offering her hand. "I run this place."

"Sass," I replied, shaking her hand. "Just arrived. What an eye opener."

"Nice to meet you. Champagne?" She signalled to the waiter for two glasses.

Chapter Thirteen

She waited patiently by the gate, knowing it could be in vain, futile. Olivia knew it was a little early but decided she would rather be outside at the gate than inside looking at the gate. Eventually it came, the hue of the dust arriving first. He handed her the bundle of mail, continuing on, the dust not even settling. She leafed hurriedly through the envelopes, searching each word, each title. With colossal disappointment she retreated back inside, the screen door banging shut behind her. "God will she ever leave," she thought. It must be soon, she was sure it was coming. But suddenly doubt crept in just like it had been for the last couple of weeks. The waiting was morphing her in to history, a set of statistics that she couldn't bear to be a part of but she had promised and Olivia knew she was good for her word. The heat made her anxious, worried, and she bit the quicks on her nails, sat down, got up again, sat down again. Sitting, she crossed her legs and jiggled her knee up and down, up and down. Her palm was covering her mouth and her fingers rested on her cheek. Nervously she wondered how long she had and kept picking at her nails. The phone rang and she jumped in terror. The landline, as her mobile had no reception out here. She rocked back and forth on the spot, summoning the courage to answer. She couldn't decide if it was better to know or not. Couldn't decide if being alerted would help. She answered; not all of her was lost yet.

"Where were you Olivia?" he demanded, knowing full well she couldn't have been far. "I was just about to hang up."

"Oh, out the back hanging out the washing," she replied casually, defying any evidence of the turmoil in her mind.

"Mmm, well maybe we need to adjust the volume so you can hear the phone wherever you are in the house."

"I will do it when I hang up," she said, diverting a crisis.

"Good. I'll be there around four - but not for long, she is feeling worse today and I must be with her."

"Of course, I understand."

"Make sure you turn that phone up and be ready for me at four." He hung up.

"Four, holy shit," Olivia thought. That did not give her long; she had been expecting him much later.

When he arrived she was ready. The music was on and the curtains were drawn. She was standing with her back to the lounge room wall. She could see herself in the mirror off to the left and smiled at the reflection. A vacant, distant smile. He opened the front door took out his camera and set it up, seeing her immediately. "Fuck," he thought every time he saw her, "she is extraordinary." He moved towards her, leaving the bag and stood directly in front of her. He was glad he installed air conditioning in the hallway of the house, only making the extreme heat mix with light spurts of cool. He could see she was only lightly sweating, happy that as per his instructions the air conditioning was only ever turned on just ten minutes before he arrived, making sure she was never too comfortable. She didn't move, knew not to. He looked at her, angry that he had missed her yesterday, his wife getting worse, not being able to escape her parents at the hospital. Olivia's toenails were glossy white and perfectly manicured and he thought of the many places he would like to see them. She had nothing on except an old oversized crop top hanging loosely off one shoulder, exposing parts of her breasts. She had her hand between her legs and he watched her fingers move in and around her cunt slowly. She moved her legs apart, allowing her other hand in, fingers everywhere hot and sweaty. Silently she moved her hand up over her stomach to where her large breasts were hanging and pulled up her top, exposing her hard nipples, palming them roughly as she groaned. Cumming in front of him, he watched.

"Don't stop," he said, "that's only one."

He took a seat on the couch, arranging his various cushions, and lit a cigarette. He thought how lucky she was to have him. Providing her with all this, glamour and opulence. Anything she wanted he brought her, let her do whatever she wanted as long as she remained in the house. She looked great on camera, better than in real life even, and the videos were going nuts. He had been so lucky to find this one, she was making him a fortune. She was lucky he had removed her from her previous life, erased that pitiful existence away and she was thankful, loved him for it. He thought about his wife now, he loved her. They couldn't have children but that had turned out to be a blessing and then she had gotten sick. Now, with the illness, she was permanently in hospital, would be until the end which was close by and that seemed to have worked out for him too. She had no idea what he got up to whilst she had been in that hospital. The father was a bit tricky, he had to be careful with him - Commissioner of the Police Force and his wife being his only daughter, only child, was full on. He couldn't believe his luck that no one had cottoned on to what he was hiding out here in this two bit town, living out his real life fantasy. She was so fucking hot.

She swayed over to him, he grabbed at her roughly between her legs, trying to fit as much of her pussy in his hand as possible. It took him one second to switch back on to her. She stiffened a little but then composed herself.

"You should be wetter than this, stickier," he complained, "running down your leg. Maybe you're getting tired of me?"

She knelt down at his crotch where his cock had grown and pulled off her shirt, shaking her breasts as she did so. He ashed onto her left tit and it fell down over her nipple. She took the cigarette from him and sucked on it deeply.

"I trust that's an indication of what's to come," he smirked. He undid his zip and released his large heavy cock from his pants. Her head moved over him, up and down, and with his free hand he stuck his fingers firmly up her arse, pulling her onto him. When he came she knew he liked to watch. She lifted her head and eyes to him, let his milky semen spill all over her mouth and face. He rubbed any she missed back across her mouth and she put her tongue out to lick at his fingers. She stood, her cunt inches away from his face, and came again for him.

"Better," he murmured, relaxing back into the couch as she fed him her cum off her fingers. By the time he had to leave she had satisfied him and the camera. He rewarded her with a giant pearl necklace and she thanked him. He told her that they loved her online. She nodded and he was gone.

She went to the table, lit a joint, smoked it and crumbled it onto the ground. She stayed there most of the night. She had no reason to move.

The next day, the same ritual. She waited by the window long enough, then moved to the front gate way too early. He came with the dust but didn't stop, kept going, the dust like always having no time to settle. She retreated inside. The phone rang, she didn't want to answer it. She answered it. He wouldn't be able to make it today, his father-in-law was coming to the hospital today, not that he needed to explain but, tomorrow, tomorrow at midday he would be there.

Tomorrow arrived with speed. She walked to the window, out to the gate. The dust came but this time it stopped, the bundle, the letter, it was there, just like she had promised one day it would be. "One day it will come," she had said, "complete with full instructions, one day." In slow motion, a catatonic state, she read, reread. The bundle. Her freedom, her way out. She had exactly three hours before he arrived. She had it all planned, down to the finer details. She had rehearsed and rehearsed. Played it out every day, praying for the day, the exact moment that it would happen. Olivia wanted to cry, to ring her rapist's wife, thank her, hug her, give her something, something to show her appreciation, her overwhelming appreciation. She loved her at this moment and always would. She had sacrificed herself for her. Her husband's slave, her husband's whore. How could she ever repay her? One day she would, one day when she had achieved all the things she had asked her to do, she would repay her. She would come back, to send him to hell for the rest of his life, like he had done to her. His wife, his beautiful, undeserving wife had saved her and she intended to spend however long it took to save her back. She knew she would never see that day, she was ill, they had told her not long. Her hero. Her guardian angel. She would die knowing what she married.

Olivia would keep her end of the bargain and crucify him, personally, all made possible by his wife, the daughter of the Police Commissioner, seeking revenge on a man she called her husband. No one would ever find out the connection, even him, her bastard husband had no idea she knew what he was doing. She had engaged the detective early on in her illness, a sense something was very wrong, things just not adding up when perhaps before she hadn't the time to ponder. It took no time. Within six months she knew his every move, his repugnant dark and sordid secret. Olivia held the papers, she couldn't believe it, confirmation of her place in the police academy. Once she had done her time, learnt everything possible, graduated at the top of class she would come back, strike, legally. Revenge: it's what they both had agreed on, the wife and the captured. What father wouldn't grant his dying daughter, only daughter, her one wish? "Accept this person into the academy no questions asked, not now, not ever. Watch over her from a distance, make sure she's okay. Do it for me daddy, before our time is over, I need to know you will make it happen." And so he had.

Olivia gripped the envelope. She had her one small bag packed for what seemed like a lifetime. Every item of worth he had ever given her, her whore money, was in there. She looked at the letter, the airplane tickets, the new passport, her new identity. Annika Osborne. She liked her already. The car arrived as the letter had said, she jumped in and disappeared like the mail, in a puff of a dust, not unlike how she arrived.

Chapter Fourteen

Audrey was fiercely ambitious. Studying at university exactly what she was told to study. She wanted to do veterinary science but that was not going to happen, not on any level, it was too humanitarian for her family so architecture it had been. Audrey's younger sister Rachel had studied medicine, a "truly great profession", and had soared through with flying colours. Audrey's father had advised her to take that course too and naturally she would, next though, if that was okay with him. There had been a huge issue to begin with that Audrey was not going to study straight away, that she might like to take a year or two off, given she was seventeen and her sisters life through a kaleidoscope, not really wanting that for herself. Rachel was seeing a barrister with an enormously successful career and an enormously huge salary. Of course they all agreed it was only a matter of time before her job soon would be to set up house, provide children and keep the home fires burning. Christian sat back and pondered. His youngest daughter was accounted for. Robert and her would have a terrific life, he would make sure of it. They were definitely going to be the most obvious to provide him with the family's legacy, sons, his grandsons. Audrey he was not so sure about. She had always tried to have a mind of her own, he had curbed it thus far but she was getting older and less easier to control. At least she had done architecture like he had firmly suggested. Who even needed pets, such a mess and a great waste of time and money.

Audrey finished her degree with honours as everyone had expected. It was her graduation night and they had just met up with her after the ceremony in the cocktail lounge. Her father had delivered a round of drinks as the fellow graduates meandered off elsewhere with their respective groups. She waved at some of her friends heading off now in a group to celebrate over dinner, leaving the families behind. Just as she was about to take her first sip Robert cleared his throat, in the dimly lit lounge and just as fast as her achievements had been celebrated they had vanished. The attention swiftly swung to Robert and Rachel as he announced their engagement. Christian embraced his son-in-law-to-be with such pride it made her flinch. Another legal mind, a great income earner with the ability to provide his daughter with the life she was accustomed to and rightfully deserved.

"And of course there's the sound of pitter-patter, the next generation, my grandson to look forward to," he laughed.

They smiled, so pleased with themselves at his blessing, at his reference to their long and fruitful life together. He hugged his graduate, commenting on how lucky a man could be, to have all of this and Christian smiled contently at his elegant wife politely sipping her champagne. The group huddled together looked from the outside impenetrable, fitted out perfectly, all behaving fabulously as one large happy family, proud parents, achieving children. Audrey stood back and prayed she could emulate the life of her adored sister, but with silent dread she knew it was not going to be easy.

After her graduation night, the family became consumed with the wedding. Naturally, Audrey was to be head bridesmaid - a job her worst enemy couldn't have given her. Still searching for a job and attending endless interviews no one seemed to notice that she had more on her plate than what colour the Egyptian paper for the invitations should be. Finally with the intervention of Christian she landed a job with a firm her father had consulted with in their lawyering arm. She didn't care how she got it, Audrey relished the diversion from the wedding and threw herself into her work. If nothing else she looked the part and was often mistaken for someone far more senior than the mere intern that she was. She wore the latest in designer fashion, sported luxury brands and drove her mother's Q Series convertible car which was hardly ever used anymore. She dated the older good-looking guys in the company but nothing ever lasted and soon she had a thing with nearly everyone there. She paved the way for almost everyone, still receiving an income from her father, assuring him that she would pay him back. Christian would joke with her, "Just find a husband, that will be pay back enough." She brought men home who were on some occasions accepted and on some occasions politely informed that the evening was over, it was getting late. Sometimes the mains had not even been served. Sadly, the balance was always difficult. The ones she liked Christian didn't, and the ones he did, they didn't like each other. She was having great trouble getting it right, knowing a partner was expected at her little sister's wedding. Her mother became more-or-less a full time aid to her sister with the wedding approaching. The corporate ladder Robert had been ambitiously climbing was paying off and invitations were appearing every second night.

Finally the big day came and went, Audrey slept with the best man but nothing further, having taken a friend from college who she had slept with years before and who now had a wonderful girlfriend.

One month after the wedding on return from their honeymoon at Audrey's birthday dinner Rachel and Robert announced their baby news.

As the grandchildren started arriving, Dorella took the role of Christian's perfectly groomed wife to the perfectly groomed grandmother with perfection, seeking attention wherever she went with her two little bundles. Sporting not only the latest looks and the sleekest figure she added the voice of wisdom and serenity to the new family unit. His beloved youngest daughter was elated and both he and Rachel relished every moment of it. Dorella sat motionless with her manicurist having the perfect manicure. No one had any idea that beneath her perfect pearls and her imported linen lay her private secret. Christian knew, but that wasn't a problem. She represented far too much to him for him to give it away. His colleagues, family and friends, loved her, thought she was the epitome of the perfect wife, a role model of motherhood and now grandmotherhood. Christian never said anything, just cleaned up the mess - like at the airport. Mostly he just looked the other way. Her son knew, but he lived in the Bahamas and they never saw him,that was what he wanted.

As Rachel's life took a hectic pace, what with mother's group, yoga for mums, book club and countless social engagements it meant that Dorella was busier than she had ever been. Of course Rachel carefully planned their social circles, only the elite were considered for a group and only exclusive invitations, often ones that impressed her father, were accepted. Christian insisted that Dorella be completely available to them, morning, noon and night, adamant that their family should not be raised by strangers when his wife was perfectly capable and absolutely available. He equally encouraged his daughter to accompany her husband at every opportunity, weekend conferences, golfing junkets in Hawaii, two weeks in Geneva - whatever it took, she shouldn't miss out, not when Dorella was there for them. His motives were simple; his daughter needed to stay as involved with her husband as possible, keep an eye on him, make sure he didn't wander and of course she was a great asset for his career. Her intelligence and attractiveness made her an ideal partner on all levels and what she lacked in humour she made up for in subtle assertiveness, gaining them great prestige in most circles. He also knew it was a great distraction for his wife. If she could fill up her days with his grandchildren, maybe she would be too tired to seek assistance at the end of the day. He had every intention to create her a new life, redefine her, knowing all too well when his second set of grandchildren arrived it would eradicate any notion of her self-indulgent ways. Surely she would feel compelled to adhere to her new grandchildren's needs like she had of the older ones. If she lost herself to his grandchildren, well, surely that was a good thing. One day she would be gone and her legacy would be his successful, confident and over-achieving heirs. Surely she wasn't selfish enough to forgo that. She was rather a disappointment to him, however unkind that seemed. Over the years she had certainly looked good and kept in good shape, but if only she had been a bit stronger, more intelligent, maybe he wouldn't have ended up with someone a little more than a trophy wife. Like his daughters, he thought, top in their classes always, graduating with honours then marrying perfectly – well, Rachel anyway. On reflection, he thought maybe he was being a bit hard. Could you ask for more than one who can converse, socialise, wear size eight, be the envy of other corporate wives or their husband's employers? Had she been more of a somebody, he thought, she probably could have generated more contacts, networked in that intelligent way, to seal the deal, get to the top. He certainly didn't believe for a moment that a girl's career was anything more than a mere stepping stone towards the right husband. Something to be proud of in the playground, something maybe to dabble in when the kids had grown, part-time. He wished his wife had found that something. She had been a dedicated hair dresser when they met but he had quickly realised she was more valuable on his arm, with her slim physique and girl-next-door good looks. She had never participated in talk about politics or war or global matters while others had, but then maybe he had encouraged her not to. That would defy the myth, the mystique of her glamour.

It was a different world now though, company men wanted some sort of opinion from their women, an educated opinion, not mere thought. He didn't understand it personally, but he saw it from the young executives who were rising up through the firm and realised the wives were starting to play a bigger role in the success of their men. He was adamant about the girls' educations, making sure they would have the credentials to marry successfully. He had raised them to be pragmatic, direct, not wishy-washy, more male-like; this was really what males wanted from their partners. He thought of his eldest daughter. She unfortunately wasn't as good looking as her sister - she was by no means unattractive but she was plain, a bit awkward, and she did herself no favours either. Her clothing was, well, what he thought was second-hand. She called it 'vintage' but to him it was someone else's hand-me-downs. She shopped like she had no money and owned nothing. He understood the artistic licence, knew he had pushed her into architecture as an alternative to interior design - or whatever she called it - but he couldn't help thinking that the reason she didn't have a steady boyfriend and no prospects was to do with her appearance. Her attitude was healthy and professional and at least at work she dressed appropriately. She achieved great success at Liquid Gold, acquiring promotion after promotion, and he couldn't deny that she had put in all the hours. She attended all of the social events, had dated some fine albeit middle-class management men, and seemed to be succeeding in the company nicely.

He couldn't put his finger on when her appearance started to change more dramatically. She stopped borrowing Dorella's convertible and started wearing her hippie clothes to work too. The relationship with her sister became strained, like they were trying to find common ground, and of course the biggest concern was that she still had no husband, not even a boyfriend. There was no doubt she loved her nieces and nephews but the sight of them would often make her wince. When Audrey announced her promotion with a transfer to Korea, there was - if he was to be honest - a sigh of relief. The dynasty he was planning, Audrey was bucking slightly, and maybe an overseas stint would be just what the doctor ordered. Of course conceptually there was also merit in having a daughter living abroad, particularly in Korea which was such a global force - a great alliance, an economy with a dynamic to match the best countries.

Dorella was at her eldest daughter's side in an instant. Travel and itineraries were her forte, spending hours researching various holiday destinations, working out logistics in the hope to lure him there quickly and efficiently. It was something he had allowed her to do, depending of course, on the attendees. Over time she had sorted out who he approved of and what countries suited him the best. Sometimes the main challenge would be convincing her companions of the need to holiday, their need to get away speaking nothing of hers. Usually it didn't take long for the women to agree and convince their husbands, knowing the trip would be top notch if Dorella was organising it.

When Audrey told her of the opportunity in Korea, she was careful not to appear too keen, but she was beside herself. The thought of getting away from her perfect daughter and their perfect bloody family and their stranglehold on her life was too overwhelming. The dream to submerse herself in Korea, particularly Korea, on her own or with her daughter - whatever it took - she couldn't let it slip away. They discussed all the good points, not really touching on the bad, and she had her daughter's bags packed before anyone could change her mind. Curiously, Christian also seemed as convinced so the move for Audrey was sealed, she had the full approval of everyone and what's more they even seemed really excited for her, for once. Dorella intended to indulge in shopping, which was never far from the cards, and try out the numerous restaurants that they were famous for. Without his prying eyes she could indulge at dinner and not worry about bills being requested and paid for, before they had even finished their first course. Dorella was sure her daughter would be fairly preoccupied, busy with relocating, settling in. Rachel suggested she should come as well to keep her mother company but Dorella had shooed her away, telling her she would be perfectly fine and would be spending most of her time attending to Audrey anyway. Concerned that she might take it up with Christian, Dorella convinced Rachel that she would be much better going with some of her girlfriends on a little holiday later, after they had found out the hot spots and the best shopping places and Dorella could even stay home with the kids whilst she had a little R & R to herself. Rachel eventually agreed, only on the proviso that the date be set for her trip. And so it was Dorella who would travel with Audrey on her big move and stay a week or maybe a little more at the most.

They arrived on schedule, checking in at the Hilton where they had booked for the first week. Audrey was eager to move into the apartment she had found online at home before they had left so with gusto they went about getting the job done. That night they had a light meal, bedding down early in preparation for the early morning start. Dorella had a glass of wine at dinner with her daughter then retired to her room.

On those first two nights in the Hilton Seoul as she said good night to her daughter she quickly called room service for more wine and drank greedily, overlooking the sparkling lights of Seoul. She had never felt so hopeless or helpless and elated at the same time. Finally a whole week to herself, more or less. She didn't want to go back, she admitted. Wandering around Seoul during the day had been absolutely liberating. How did she end up here? Drunk and sad, just so, so sad. She knew alcohol lead to self-pity, knew it was a depressant and that suited her perfectly. She was depressed, that was for sure. But it wasn't because of alcohol. It was ultimately her fault, she knew. She let him win and with every winner there was a loser. That was her real title: "loser". She knew it and she knew he thought it too. He knew she drank and yet he never said a thing. When he would come home late from work, from boardroom meetings, she knew he checked the trash, checked the fridge. Often found water, not wine in the bottles. Still nothing. Like he was dead, like she was dead to him. Not a word, she was grateful, thankful, she couldn't give it up but deep down it made it worse. It was the one thing that was hers, she owned it solely and it made her not so god damn perfect; flawed. She ordered and ordered on those two nights, not once looking back. She blamed jetlag on the first morning and then flu from the cold air conditioning on the second. She was fulfilling her end of the bargain, doing her motherly duties as she had promised, just with huge hangovers. She was an old woman, she reminded her daughter, feeling much older than she was even as she said it. Her insides were worn out, cracked, but her daughter bought it and she got away with it, so much so that she drank again the following night. Her youngest daughter was at least more like her, definitely enjoyed a drink - not on her scale, but it was nice all the same to go to her house and find wine in the fridge. Her friends were also partial to a drink, some more than others but then, she was more again. She knew that when the party stopped for them, it stopped, they didn't pick it back up when they got home or drink quiet vodkas to block out the silence. She kept liquor in some of her mineral water bottles in one of the bar fridges. Their house was an entertaining house with absolutely no shortage of fridges, cold-rooms, cellars. It was easy to hide, just a nip here and there. It seemed right to her to be indulging this way, in Korea on her own. She barely knew who she was now but had vivid ideas of who she had been. She resented her youngest daughter for bringing her children into her life. She was at their mercy, beck and call, and she resented it. He perpetuated it, encouraged and enforced it. She knew he was trying to fill up her dance card. Keep her schedule tight, responsible. If anyone needed to be picked up after dinner it was her job. There was no discussion. She picked those kids up from all over town. It didn't matter that there were other hours in the day. She was terrified that she might get pulled over and random-breath-tested. That would be inexcusable, even to her. She didn't need to sing it from a rooftop. But here, on her own, she let it consume her, wrap itself around her and drown her in it.

The flight home was equally satisfying. She knew she had two legs and proceeded to enjoy the fruits of the mini bar after take-off. She landed in Singapore for a two-hour connection flight and made her way to the Platinum Room piano lounge. As she boarded the final flight for home, a quick check meant she had another two to three hours of drinking before she could sleep if off for the arrival. No one the wiser. Unfortunately she fell asleep almost immediately after her first drink. When she woke, she was angry with herself for the mistake. She checked again - still three or four hours before landing. Certainly enough time to sober up if she took it slowly. She ordered a bottle of chardonnay and before she knew it was finishing her third. She asked for one more glass and the stewardess politely informed her that they were preparing for landing and the bar had closed. She leant back into her seat, feeling the ceiling around her swirl. She closed her eyes, which made it worse. She tried to get up but couldn't work her fastened seatbelt. She became agitated with the belt, angry and impatient. She screamed at someone that the seat belt was broken and began a torrent of abuse about her safety, how stuck she was and what if the plane crashed or lost the use of its engines, how would she survive? Hysterically she screamed, "I am going to die in this seat!" She was still pulling ferociously at the belt. Others started to assist; the stewards, other passengers, but no one could get close. An elderly gentleman approached.

"Dorella? Dorella Brown? It's Terry Anderson, I am a colleague of your husband, Christian."

She gazed over at the mention of his name, he leant in and unhooked her belt. She got up and roughly pushed past him, heading for the toilets. She stumbled as she went, steadying herself with the backs of the seats. Just as her hand grabbed the handle she threw up onto the floor of the toilet, plunging in after it. She shut the door, leaning against it, seeing nothing, just blurs, a mesh of cold surfaces. It was how she felt; cold, removed. Like the cubicle. She bent over to the toilet, stepping over the mess on the floor, and sat on the lid. She closed her eyes, trying to pull herself together. She relaxed, letting the adrenaline go and drifting off. In the distance she heard banging and calling, maybe on a door – it was too far away for her to bother with. She curled up on the ground beside the toilet, tiredness overwhelming her, falling asleep again.

The next thing she knew she was getting out of her seat, the plane had landed and she was being escorted down the platform towards the arrival gates. She was past caring, her façade had finally cracked. She needed help and maybe now she would get it. There were thoughts of relief of the charade being over. She felt for the first time in decades calm, hopeful, saved.

He saw her approaching, a steward on either arm. She looked terrible, ill, sick. He looked around to see if he knew anyone, a witness, or how many people were noticing her. No one looked obvious as he headed towards her and she leant helplessly into his body.

"She's had a bit too much to drink, Mr Brown. Nothing serious, got a bit excited, that's all," the steward explained casually with a huge smile.

Christian stared at him. "Thank you so much. Sorry, I didn't catch your name?"

"Peter," the flight attendant answered, "Peter Stanford."

"Well Mr Stanford, much thanks for looking after my wife. I can understand," he grinned, "she doesn't drink and flying scares her senseless. Our daughter is in Korea and unfortunately this is her only means of transport. I usually fly with her but I had a sudden meeting I had to attend. Poor thing, she assured me she would be fine. I'll know better next time. Again, thank you so much. I'll make sure to send an email."

She murmured something and he held her close, not the slightest bit interested, knowing he wouldn't understand it anyway.

"We'll be off then, sorry for the hassle." He shook Peter's hand with a hundred dollar bill snug inside, passing it to him.

"What a jerk," Peter thought, but accepted his money and headed back to the aircraft. "The bloody rich," he thought, "they're all the same, alcoholics and arseholes."

Christian turned to escort her away when a man called his name, "Christian!" He saw him just as he said his name and smiled broadly.

"Coming or going Terry?"

"Coming Christian, actually just got off the same flight as your wife."

Dorella nodded at him and smiled weakly.

"Ahh, so how do you feel? The flight attendant said she may have had food poisoning, she was apparently quite crook up there."

Terry looked at them both and shook his head. "Must have missed me. But I don't generally eat airplane food, looks like it's finally paid off."

Christian agreed and steered the conversation to work. After a quick brief, they parted company, Terry kindly patting Dorella's arm as he left. He would drink too if he was married to that smug man.

"Rachel?" Dorella murmured at the car, "why are you here?"

"Long story mum," Rachel said with concern, "Dad's dropping off to get my car which is just around the corner. Are you alright? You look terrible!"

"Food poisoning! Can you believe it. First class, you don't expect this sort of thing. I'll be dealing with it tomorrow, don't you worry Dorella, they'll be hearing from me," said Christian.

Nothing was said the entire drive home. He dropped Rachel off to pick up her new car and ran Dorella a bath when they got in.

"You must be exhausted after such an ordeal, not to mention the actual flight as well. I wonder what you ate," he said, more to himself than her, confirming the story. He knew how well they were looked after when they flew and was sure the situation was well-contained, under control, no one on the flight being any the wiser. He should probably follow up with a letter, he thought, and made a mental note to instruct his PA in the morning. That would give it some legs. Quite happy with himself he opened a mineral water and sat down to flick on the news. "We'll let this pass," he thought, smiling, knowing the good behaviour she would be on for some time given the incident. He thought he'd send a little something to Terry too, maybe a pre-packaged sandwich - something to make a joke of airplane food. When he finally went to check on her she was curled up in bed fast asleep. Tomorrow would be better. He phoned for flowers to arrive in the morning. She loved flowers and he had an early start, so best to leave her something for when she woke up.

She awoke with a groan, her head thumping, pounding. There were flowers beside her bed and the smell made her gag. Where had they come from? "Oh god, I hope they weren't welcome home flowers," she thought. She cried. What happened? Well, she knew what physically had happened, but why and what now? Nothing? A bath, bed, flowers? Didn't they tell him? She swore they told him, said she had too much to drink. Maybe they didn't? It was a blur, she admitted. Relieved that there was no one around she rolled back into the covers. Lay there trying to piece the mess together. After a while she had to get up to get paracetamol, serapax, something for her head.

Did that mean she was drinking gin? Her head felt more like a gin hangover than wine. She knew it wasn't vodka, didn't get bad hang overs on vodka, which was why she drank it. She started to recall, definitely gin on the first leg and in the Platinum Room, but couldn't be sure of the final stretch. She knew there was wine, lots of wine. She jumped up abruptly at the image of herself screaming about her seat belt. Literally assaulting people to get them off her, away from her. Oh Christ, that man, Tom - or Tim? - someone who knew Christian. Would he tell? Here she was, a fifty-year-old woman, thinking "did he tell", like that was the biggest issue. Did they see him afterwards? What did it matter, the damage was done. Terrified, she sat on the edge of her bed. She began to panic; a slow internal panic, one that spread like cancer through her bones until it overwhelmed her. Her hands were covering her mouth in fear. There was no going back, he wouldn't ignore this.

Chapter Fifteen

I liked her instantly, her eyes and smile were kind. The champagne arrived and I glanced at her with a stranger's nod, noticing again how beautiful she was. Her huge almond-green eyes were so sad yet so happy and her long refined neck met a perfectly oval face that made her eyes loom out from under their lashes. Her high angular cheekbones mirrored the length of her wide yet sombre smile. She had well-kept honeyed-blonde hair, straight and long. Trying to tidy myself, I smoothed down my dress, adjusted my straps and wished fervently I had at some stage brushed my teeth. Her skin was smooth and the fine lines around her mouth and eyes gave away nothing. We exchanged niceties, as people do, not knowing each other and I thanked her profusely for the champagne.

"Is it Laurent Perrier?" I enquired.

"Yes," she answered, surprised. "You obviously know your wines."

We got into a lengthy discussion about champagne and champagne houses, favourites and not-so-favourites. When our glasses were both drained Annika asked if I would like to meet up for dinner at one of the island's favourites. It was for locals only, she said, not cool enough for tourists. She went every Wednesday, confessing she was a bit of a creature of habit and that well, today was Wednesday. Her night off. She smiled that smile again.

"It's completely safe, you're completely safe," Annika said. "I'm a police officer actually, not trying to hit on you."

Laughing, the thought actually not ever entering my mind, I explained that that made two of us, just without the policewoman part.

"My kids would think it was amazing, going to dinner with a police officer. My youngest is obsessed," I explained.

I don't know why I told her that, maybe to reaffirm my position, or maybe just to speak their names, tell someone of their existence. I told her I would love to come, she'd be doing me a favour by letting me get away from the backpacker scene for a moment and pretend to be back in the real world. She said she'd come and get me from the hostel at six. The restaurant was too hard to find on your own. We agreed on the time and she headed back into the cafe.

By the time the night was over a bond was formed like nothing we had ever known and least of all expected. The night had started off casually enough, but within the hour all the stones had been overturned. Annika reminded me of someone I once knew, my husband. She was a great listener, sharp and intelligent yet compassionate and considerate. She was damaged too, the small glimpses of pain that dulled in her eyes revealed the trauma's and ordeal's she had been through, was in. We had ended in tears, trembling, holding each other close, the unlocking of the sorrow and sadness and the huge amount of self-pity (mainly on my side) a relief. The remoteness, the complete anonymity of it all, both of us brand new, no knowledge, no data, had somehow, somewhere propelled us both, into an grave honesty.

Her face and voice were unjudging, it was such a relief, I hadn't intended to confide so much, admit so much but she was warm and encouraging, empathetic, like she knew, understood. The trust flooded and thinking back, it knew it had happened in the cafe the moment I met her.

We were like two sister souls coming from different places but for the same reasons, Annika and Sassy, lost but hoping to be found. She told me many things that night; there was much behind her façade. She had been badly treated, became a cop to repay a favour and repay the favour she did. But now she couldn't find her next step, didn't know who or what she had become. She envied in a caring way that I still had motherhood, as a title to define me, distract others from really wondering who I was, what I did, what I stood for. I agreed completely but confided quietly that sometimes it just served as a band-aid, the title 'mum' used sometimes as an excuse to opt out of yourself, to not have to look or question or query anything bigger than parenting, to just exist in the form of a mother.

"Wow, look at the time." I leant back, exhausted. "Two A.M. Do they often leave you here to lock up?" I enquired finally, not giving it any thought when the waiter threw her the keys.

"Never," she said, "in fact I didn't even really register they were doing that but you're right, it's just us. I'll drop them off after I take you home, they live in my street."

"I leave tomorrow, it doesn't seem right only just having met you. It's strange, it's like we're lovers in an affair."

"Oh, it's nothing like that." Annika said calmly. "It's so much more. I've never had this feeling with anyone in my entire life Sass, it feels like I've known you forever. I don't want to weird you out, but you know what I mean?"

"I do, Annika. It's like talking to my sister talking to you, and that's serious. How about coffee tomorrow? We'll talk more then. I mean, I'm only a three-hour flight away. What about Christmas, Easter, your birthday? Anything. Let's make an occasion to meet again."

"Yep, we'll sleep on it and then tomorrow – coffee, a swim and me coming to you!"

"Awesome, I can't wait to introduce you to everyone and then convince you to move. I can't have met another sister just to lose her again. If that's one thing I've learnt, it can all be gone in a moment."

Linking arms, we headed to her car and laughed about the restaurant's owners.

"We should have got sozzled in there!" Annika exclaimed. "Can you imagine, the island finding us passed out drunk on the floor from the night before. I'd have to leave!" she laughed.

"Mmm, I don't even think we touched that bottle of wine, did we? The confessions took over."

"You're right Sass, what a night. I can't tell you how happy I am that I ran into you today. It was a new moon you know, it was meant to be."

"Absolutely Annika, absolutely."

With a huge weight lifted from my shoulders, a weight that had been there for so long I had thought it could never be removed, I rang the children and talked to them excitedly about my return only two days away, and the new friend I had made. They sounded happy and content, keen to see me, they said as they rushed onto their day's activities and what Poppy and Grandma were cooking for dinner. I was glad for them, so proud of them that they had managed to become the beautiful thoughtful children that we had both hoped for. I knew they had changed, I knew their hearts were broken like mine but somehow they managed to put it in its place - a skill I was still trying to work on.

The next day was spent lazily catching up with Annika, so happy to be in her company. We talked like school-girls, scheming and devising plans to hook up again. We agreed on her birthday, she would come to visit, meet my kids, my family, stay with me and dine at my restaurant. She confided that her dream was to become a chef and when we met for coffee that morning she told me she had finally done it, enrolled that morning in an apprenticeship on the mainland. She was going to sell her cafe and do it, become a chef.

"Look out," she said, "in a year's time I'll be cooking for you somewhere."

Thrilled for her I agreed, eagerly arranging the next soiree after her birthday to be at her restaurant. We laughed excitedly. I told her I could just see it: Yes chef, oui chef! We hugged tightly as I left, not wanting to let go. I couldn't thank her enough for what she had unknowingly given me. She said it was the other way around. I texted her on the flight before we took off: "Thank you again my dear friend. You have thrown me a lifeline, you are in my heart now and forever. I simply cannot wait until your birthday in six months. Start chopping girlfriend! X."

Chapter Sixteen

Nothing much had changed since Audrey left. She hadn't expected it to. This was not her first visit home. She had been back and forth a number of times since she moved and nothing much had changed then. her girlfriend's Fortieth, the birth of another niece, friends' weddings. There were many occasions, "all for everyone else" she thought as she sat in the back of her father's Mercedes, Dorella in the front. The quietness in the car was hurting her ears and she wished they would say something. She knew she had to face it sometime. "Why can't they bring it up?" she mused. Why did they always remain resolute to being so perfect. To avoid disappointment at all costs. Growing silently angry, she realised that their whole lives had been spent avoiding the tasteless periods of reality. She didn't want to admit to herself more than anyone that she should have known better. Deep down she knew she said yes to please her father, to fit in to the family mould, not stick out, not be discussed with a sigh in her father's voice. He was nice, her fiancée, very nice and after two years of dating it was the next step. The truth was when she considered the alternative, considered what her father would say if she turned him down, rejected potentially the only opportunity of someone asking her to marry her, it was too much so she had said yes to keep her father happy. He had been so happy, so proud when she announced their engagement to her parents. The main emotion she knew her father was feeling was relief. Relief that he could stop making excuses for her, relief that he could include her in the 'we' statements, relief that family holidays would have even numbers not odd. She made a resolution to no longer care about what he thought of her previously, to put it behind them all and soak up all the attention everyone was lavishing on her. Her mother even seemed to change with the news. She walked with purpose, straightened her shoulders, smiled. "Constantly smiling" her sister told her, said it had done their mum a world of good. The reaction and response from everywhere, everyone had convinced her that she had done the right thing. Finally she was in the group, finally she was one of them and she felt people's perception of her actually change. "Maybe there is nothing wrong with her after all" she imagined people saying, "maybe she is just like her successful married sister." She rolled with it, embraced it and drank it all up. Finally it was her turn under the disco ball and she loved every single minute of it.

The problem was, she didn't really love every single minute with him. He sort of bored her, there was no challenge, no passion, no fire. By the end, after three long years where she knew it wouldn't change, she said yes - and now the humility. Not even did she get to a failed marriage, just a failed wedding with a huge bill. Everyone was supportive, calm, stoic.

Christian suggested that she come home for good, said Korea was not where she should be. She thought he was trying to protect her, have her close after such an ordeal - until he mentioned the lovely man who had just joined them in the firm. He was single too and would be perfect for her. He joked that maybe she should keep the honeymoon booking just in case. She quickly realised his motives were not from love and concern but from fear and despair. She had no fight left anyway. She agreed to pack up and return and her mother arranged everything swiftly. In turn, the perfect man abruptly left the firm; his mother had fallen ill and there was a tumour, three months left to live. So here she sat, looking out the window of her parents car, waiting for the 'what next', knowing it would come.

Book Two

Chapter One

I thought about the offer again, for the last time. Even now I find it difficult to recall what was real and what was fiction, it had gone on for so long. The buyer had pestered and pestered, I remember that, sent numerous emails until finally I called his bluff and accepted. Unbelievably, he hadn't flinched. Six months of harrowing relentlessness for him, the result always predictably the same and now in the blink of an eye with no explanation, a win. I said yes out of the blue, out of nowhere and yet still he showed nothing. Calm, receptive, like he always knew I would cave. The contract was drawn up and the offer was sealed. By then the offer was well overpriced and too good to refuse, he agreed that he had fallen in love with it and wanted it. The one downside was that he was taking my business partner, my friend, my chef with him. He insisted the chef stay on and to my shock the chef wanted to. Manny was kind and gentle as he let me down, slowly explaining that he couldn't do another one, his heart wasn't in it anymore. He had lost the enthusiasm but hadn't wanted to lose me. He vowed he loved being in business with me, couldn't deny he had made good money with me and, sobbing, knew there would be nothing else like it again for him. He knew what he was giving up, not even sure if he was doing the right thing, how could he? Was he mad? But there it was, even with all that he had to stop, slow down. He was so sorry but if I decided to sell the restaurant he would prefer to stay on with the new owner and, yes, end the long-term partnership that worked so well. I told Manny I would refuse his offer to take the restaurant. I told him I wouldn't go it alone and if he didn't want to do another restaurant then together we would stay put. No sale but something had changed. The relationship had changed and slowly we acknowledged, the chef and I, that we wanted different things. Now we both knew where we really stood and there was no going back. I loved him like a brother but I realised the honeymoon was over and it was time to go our own ways. Adamant not to destroy what we had by carrying on longer than a partnership should, I signed the contract to sell our restaurant. Manny would stay on and we would stay mates.

I had found a new business partner, my best friend and the site we were going to take was definitely another winner. I found myself feeling tired and, flat and wondered if in fact all I needed was a break, a small change, maybe not a complete departure from it all but a getaway none the less. It was too late, I had sold the restaurant and signed the lease on the new one - but could I still get away, take a break? The restaurant in Paris that Thierry and I had built after Tom had passed away had been ticking along perfectly. With Thierry in charge running the show, but maybe I could've relocated and taken the kids to live in France. It was what Tom and I had always dreamed of. The kids loved it there, I loved it there. What if starting another restaurant was a bad idea? Maybe I should have just slowed down. Annika came, I invited her. I couldn't go back on the deal now. We were committed and I was sure I was just a little stressed.

An email beeped at me from Thierry, always like he is psychic. "Looks like we are on target Sass, are you still coming in June? We will be ready. Joseph wants to talk also. Can you call him? T."

Thierry, my mind sank back into the day we met Thierry. Warm, sunny typical weather. He had strolled into our restaurant, lazily perching at the bar and enquiring, "Do you need a chef?". I had replied equally as flippantly 'Who doesn't need a chef in hospitality?" especially a French one, I thought quietly.

I couldn't wait until June. France, that's where I needed to be now. Annika would handle the new restaurant. I grabbed my phone.

Chapter Two

The weather today made it much easier to depart. Normally warm and sunny, the city was grim and bleak - somewhat appropriate for my arrival in to France for this time of the year. I glance down at my wedding rings, smiling, remembering this day fifteen years ago, the weather outside exactly the same. So much for global warming and weather change. It had been an outstanding wedding despite the miserable weather. We'd had 150 guests in a marquee perched on the top of the city. There'd been fireworks, DJs, a pianist, a live band, course after course, champagne after champagne and loads of singing and dancing. It was a festival, carnival, we had both seen to it and everyone had been in full flight. No arguments, no squabbling, great mates and great wine. Now, today was my wedding anniversary and by pure coincidence here I was sitting at the same airport, fifteen years on with fifteen years past. I bet France hadn't changed the way I had since we last met.

Charles de Gaulle is the second busiest airport in Europe, to Heathrow. Our landing was seamless as was the flight and the hundreds of various movies to choose from had made time fly. I was glad my French had vastly improved since last time - not that that would have been difficult given I was only just managing a "Merci".

"Bonjour Madame, welcome to Paris," a lady spoke to me as I approached the ticket station.

"Bonjour, ca va?" I asked, probably too informally for the occasion, but the other options seemed too formal.

"Tres Bien Madame, comment allez- vous, did you have a good flight?"

"Oui, merci, it was no problem."

"J' voudrais un billet pour Montparnesse s'il vous plait," I asked.

"Oui Madame, 16.50 merci."

I took the ticket and went back to my luggage. The sun was coming up, it was early and the fog was gently clearing. I pulled out my hat and scarf and, rugging up, left the warmth of the airport lounge and headed into Paris. The chill made my hands numb within minutes but the fresh air was a welcome from twenty-four hours of flying and confined regurgitated air.

"Madame, your ticket please." Was it me or was there more English around than last time?

"Oui, monsieur," I answered. "The weather is good today, no?" I asked.

"Oui Madame, this is tres bien. Last week it was snowing!"

I nodded a look of surprise at him and agreed that this was indeed better. I was definitely not packed for snow.

As usual the coach into Paris took over two hours but I was infinitely glad that I had chosen the bus over the taxi. The taxis in Paris were a rip-off at the best of times, let alone when they sight a foreigner from the airport. The coach was fairly empty, only eight of us in total, so I took the back seat and stretched out my legs. Like all airports the scenery that greeted you upon arrival and followed you through, from the large anticipation filled terminals, to the main outside arterial almost always connected you with unfulfilling and uninspiring first impressions, compounded with an anxiety that makes you think twice about the destination that you so stoically fought for. The surrounds were always the same. Low lying areas stacked with industry and housing commissions. Paris was no different. Of course it was the most beautiful city in the world, for me, but still for a good hour after leaving the airport the area's surrounds were bleak. I couldn't help but look eagerly around, even though it was somewhat familiar to me, and study the monuments and buildings we passed. Images filled my mind of the second world war, of occupied France and I realised I was shivering in the heat of the coach.

I started reading WWII books when I was ten after a year of recurring dreams in which I was part of the resistance in occupied France. I would wake up and swear that my Nazi uniform was hanging on the back of my bedroom door only to find it never there. My parents dismissed it but I would argue that my dreams were real, that clearly it was my previous life, my reincarnation. Laughing, they would pat me on the back and agree, moving on with their business in the world we lived in. I knew I had to seek help elsewhere so at lunchtime at school I would head to the library and devour any literature I could find on occupied France. Soon my interest grew from intrigue to obsession, and still now I often read stories of the war and all that they encompassed. As we nudged along in peak hour traffic I could see the soldiers lining the banks, the trees stripped bare of any life, like so many at that time, and the shots went off in my head. It was the same every time I left Charles de Gaulle.

My hotel room was available when I arrived at Rue de Stanlisas in the St Germain and the concierge showed me through.

"Welcome back Madame, your flight was good, all things considered?"

"It is the same every time no? Just a means to an end, to get me back in Paris. How are you Martin? Business is good, the hotel is full?"

"No Madame, we are much quieter this year than last. We can blame many things but we know the truth is in our nation's leadership, or should I say lack of."

"Ahh," I responded, "this was not popular. What a shock for him to succeed. The country is furious, no? Having said that, Martin, someone had to vote for him. He won did not he not?"

"Oui Madame, that he did and now we will reap the benefits of an even more fallen economy. Restaurants are closing down faster than they are opening and the tourists are arriving less and less. You are lucky Restaurant6 is still doing well. Thierry has quite a reputation."

"Merci Martin, but you are right, we are lucky."

Once up in my room I unpacked my bags and ran the bath. A glass of Chateauneuf de Pape was already poured by the bath's edge and I smiled to myself at the routine I had gotten myself into. A knock at the door turned me around and I wondered what I had forgotten. Wrapping the bathrobe around myself I opened the door.

"I am so sorry Madame, but we are experiencing some trouble with the hot water. Martin has asked to apologise for not mentioning it but we are expecting it back on in an hour or two. Please should you wish to take your bath at our neighbouring hotel, Martin will organise it."

"Non, merci, pas den probleme. Please could you bring me du fromage?"

"Of course Madame I will organise it now."

What a pain. I lay back on the bed, flicking the remote control on the TV. My cheese arrived within moments and I turned on the news channel. Wine and cheese at nine A.M. was so indulgent and I loved every minute of it. The news was as I expected, not very lively, but fashion week had just ended in Paris and the commentators were reliving every moment. Pictures of haute couture flashed across the screen and Donatella Versace was on the arm of Prince Harry. "A huge success," the news reporter was saying. Buyers were flocking in from all over to pick up the designs. The phone rang in the room.

"Bonjour?' I said. "Merci Martin I will." The hot water was fixed; the problem was not so bad.

It was not long before I was on Rue de Rennes heading towards the Seine, people were fussing everywhere in the typical French way, rushed, off hand, busy. They were aware there was no city like Paris and owned it like it was their own child. "Excuse-moi, excuse-moi," they muttered as they slightly knocked me on the street in their bid to get by. It's no problem," I say but no one is listening. Walking along the Seine, the weather whilst clear is still chilly and I rub my hands together inside my gloves. I could see the Eiffel Tower now and hugged myself, picking up my pace towards Rue de New York. The river was empty this morning; the houseboats had gone south for the winter and it was too early for tourist boats yet. The tour d'eiffel loomed ahead and I walked towards it, keeping it in sight. I didn't know what it was but it was true the effect of the most famous monument in the world was majestic. Even thinking of it now I tried to pull apart the pieces. I broke it down to balustrading, to steel, to construction, to usefulness, but even then I was still mesmerised. It was my favourite, my absolute favourite picture in the world. The Eiffel Tower was worthy of all of its success, all its power, all it embodied. There was simply nothing else that even came close to its marvellousness. It was what dreams were made of and no matter how objectively you considered the Tower it still was monumental, and not just for its formation. I crossed the du point over to the right bank, shivering a little as the chill set in. The leaves were all gone on the trees and the Seine was silently sitting. Out of habit I dropped a coin over the side and watched it land metres and metres below. The traffic had thinned for mid-morning but would return soon for the lunch hour. I contemplated bringing cigarettes as Paris was the only place I still smoked but had decided against it. But now as people brushed past me alongside I eagerly inhaled the smell, licking my lips, craving for one. I would find a cigarette at the restaurant so I hurried myself, I could see the awning in the distance. Crossing over to the front of the restaurant, a taxi flew by, almost taking out a motorbike and the driver screamed something at him but the wind carried it up into the air. I nodded in his direction to show my distaste but it too was lost to the atmosphere. The lights were on through the sheer curtains and I pushed open the heavy timber doors, grateful to be entering warmth.

He was sitting there, kind and complex, a cigarette hanging loosely from his lips. His eyes turned to me and he raised his eyebrows. Not a smile, not a hello - just a look, an acknowledgement, he was expecting me. He was writing in his little red book, legs casually crossed at the ankles as they stretched out past the base of the table. His ashtray was next to a lamp on the small table, half-filled and an empty espresso cup sat off to the right. It was still grey outside, the sun not yet broken through the overcast clouds but in here, through the shimmer of the asparagus coloured sheer curtains, Paris looked full of colour. The Eiffel Tower appeared to stand perfectly in the far corner of the room, the windows made purposefully to frame it. I looked at it, like everyone did who walked through this door and breathed out, loving the view, loving the effect it had in the room, there but only there, when you actually look. It was as if it was an afterthought, my beloved Tower. The room so elegant and peaceful. And then there in the corner the Eiffel Tower for all to see. Some could mistake it for being purely a picture until you noticed the cars moving around like ants at the base and the lights spraying the structure every hour.

"Coffee?" he asked.

"Oui Monsieur," I smiled.

His long frame stood and effortlessly he walked around the bar. Time was not a consideration, he moved always the same: slowly, elegantly. Even in the kitchen there was no rush, everything was done with thought, finesse, like it was the last dish he may ever make. I envied his ability to ignore time, ignore reality.

"How was your trip? I would have collected you from the airport you know," he said.

"You are good Thierry. The coach is simply less fuss and I get to take my walk, arrive under her spell. Thanks all the same," I replied.

"Ahh, it's not as impressive as you make out. Your love affair with that thing amuses me."

"Oui oui oui, I have heard it all before. It's my love affair, leave it alone."

"As you want," he said with finality, passing me the coffee and kissing me from cheek to cheek.

"We need another induction cooker, I have one on order if you agree," he asked.

"The numbers are growing eh? You are happy? The feedback is great, you're doing an amazing job. You do as you need. You know I trust you."

"We have more to do but merci, I appreciate the comment. Pierre has left us. I'm not altogether too unhappy, he was thin amongst the team. I have a replacement to start next week. I will introduce you while you're here. Stephane, he will be better."

I nodded and opened a bottle of Perrier. "Sounds good. We've had a Stephane before, not the same I assume?"

"No, very different," he answered with his serious and indignant tone.

"How long are you here for?" he asked as I took a seat opposite him and nodded in the direction of his cigarettes.

"Two weeks, give or take. I have to head south to St Tropez to see Christelle, but I'm not sure when I will go. There are obviously a few things we need to do here with the new facade and the new wine cellar opening, but apart from that it's just routine. How are you placed? Do you want to come south or is it too hard?'

"Mmm not sure. I will see where I'm at when you go. I would like to see Christelle also, so maybe it will work. Has she had the baby?"

"No, she is due any minute though. I think she is panicking a little but she will be perfect, as she is with everything."

"Reminds me of someone else," he commented.

"Why, was that a compliment Thierry? You mustn't indulge me so," I smiled.

"You've had a long flight, it's the least I can do," he replied stoically.

"No need chef, the flight is the least of my ailments," I matched his stoic tone.

"Ouch," he replied.

"Are we going to lunch? Are Isabel and Antoine coming?" I enquired, thoroughly enjoying my cigarette, wondering why on earth I didn't just take it back up again permanently.

"We are booked at Septime, but Isabel is too busy, lunch is full today. She will join us later. Antoine is coming, I will pick him up. Should I collect you too?"

"No honey, I will meet you there. Joseph is expecting me, I don't know how long he will take. I don't want to keep you waiting." Joseph our beloved friend, Tom mine and Thierry could sometimes get lost in his world of figures and I was sure given I had only just arrived the catch up chat would have to happen too. Even though he was employed as our accountant he was so much more than that, to everyone I was connected to.

"You are the main attraction, we will wait as long as we have to."

I touched his shoulder and leant over to give him a kiss on the cheek. "You are the main attraction from all reports. I have to run, see you in an hour."

I left him with his cigarette in his mouth, making his notes for the day, and stepped out into the chilly Parisian air. The crispness was welcoming from the warmth of the room but I knew the feeling wouldn't last and I'd be back to icy cold by the time I'd taken two steps. I pulled my hat down low over my ears and stretched out my fingers in my gloves. I looked back at the Eiffel Tower as I headed in the opposite direction and hailed a taxi, blowing a kiss in its wake.

I had been coming to Paris for ten years now. We opened Restaurant6 the year after Tom died; I needed a change, something to take my mind off my life. It had been our dream to be amongst the French, to raise our children with France in their lives. We travelled annually to maintain the relationship, to keep in the loop of the culinary science. We made it our business to know intimately the workings of a French restaurant. We had owned enough restaurants to understand the fundamentals but Paris was an art, one that needed a much more refined skill. A tough city and a tough game. Still, it had been our dream and we had spent years learning and listening. A restaurant in Paris, it was what we worked so hard for.

Thierry was instrumental. From Paris and passionate to own his own restaurant, the partnership had evolved. He started with us six years earlier, had been our Head Chef through various restaurants until three years ago when his desire to return home overcame him, luckily Matty had stepped up and been able to take over for him, the two of them good good friends starting out with us together. Thierry was Parisian to the core and his homesickness became too much. We sat down with him, tried to convince him to stay but the calling was too strong. We did however all decide that one day we would work again together - not as the chef and the owners, but as business partners, equals setting the world on fire. We established a restaurant fund and contributed to it monthly. We declared when we had a million dollars we would begin, until then he would immerse himself back in the Paris society and keep his ears to the ground for the right opportunity. When Tom died we were a hundred thousand dollars short of our aim but somehow between us, without a word spoken, the restaurant became urgent and we secured a site six months later. It took six months to fit out, to organise and to open and Thierry did it all, with professionalism and efficiency. We had a contract written up outlining exactly how the partnership was going to work and yet we never once had to refer to it.

It wasn't long before the restaurant took off and the critics loved it. He was their new 'in-chef'. He took the position seriously and played the game seriously. The result had made him even more liked. A French chef without the arrogance, without the playboy attitude, he became unique and somewhat sought after. He started to see Marie, a lawyer-turned-model who lived not far from the restaurant. She came in one night to inspect the fuss and Thierry had had a shocker in the kitchen. She heard his tirade on her way to the bathroom and was intrigued by the brutality of him, given the neat and tidy image the press had painted of him. Always liking the bad guys, she sent him a drink at the end of the night to say thank you for such an outstanding meal. He sent a polite thank you note back but nothing further. Curious, she attended the following week, repeating her first performance with another drink sent at the end of the meal and the result was the same again, a polite thank you. By her fifth visit, Thierry sent out five complimentary courses to get in first and match the five drinks.

It cemented the relationship. They were invited to all the events and seen around the city week in and week out, the couple were a true Parisian item and seemingly madly in love. As a shock to all after two years they split; the long hours he worked had become a bore to her and the weekends where she was used to partying, he was used to working. She was sick of arriving solo and before too long she was seen repeatedly not departing solo. It was not long after their break-up that she started to see another chef at Chez George. He was a little older than Thierry and more established so he could come and go as he pleased from his kitchen. With her in tow, some twelve months after they started dating the two of them moved south to Biarritz and opened Bistro M. Twelve months later, she was back in Paris, word was with a partner in a law firm and expecting their first child.

When I arrived at Joseph's, he had his head down on the phone so I made myself comfortable in the den. It was not long before he hung up.

"Sasskia, how wonderful it is to see you. You really must start to visit Paris far more often. This three times a year is ludicrous, you bring such vibrancy into our dull Parisian lives."

"Ah, Joseph, it is wonderful to see you again also. You look terrific, something Dora has had a hand in?"

"No my Sass, can you believe I have decided to do the London Marathon at fifty-five-years-old? And my trainer is adamant he won't lose me. He has me on a tyrant of a training schedule and we are only three months in. The marathon is another year away but alas, you know how I am. Set my mind to it and It's fait accompli."

"Well it looks like it's doing you a world of good. I've never seen you look better and that's saying something, given the outstanding shape you've always kept yourself in."

Joseph laughed, "I love how you arrive with your immediate compliments. It's so un-French! It's a national sport here to put everyone down. Do sit."

We looked through the books over de menthe tea, a homemade speciality of Dora's his beautiful wife. He looked at me seriously.

"Sass, the business is really going well. The whole team is doing a marvellous job. The renovations will come in under budget, as Thierry has kept an astute eye on them and the result already seems to be impressive. You received my email last week with the article from Le House. The diners are just lapping it up. Dining in the Cave is going to be extraordinary and there's a real buzz around.

'It does seem though that we are going to go over schedule. The final works won't be done for at least another two months so for now, you are at the hands of the builders and you have your new restaurant in New York to take care of also. I know you were hoping to be of more help for this visit but really, Thierry and Carrie are right on top of it. There is very little left for you to do except to come back in a couple of months for the final inspection." Joseph sighed at me and spread his hands on his table.

"Mmm, I was hoping that wouldn't be the case but I had considered it. I was at the restaurant this morning and I could see it wasn't near finished. I guess the good part is the delay is at the cost of the builders, not me. I will talk with Thierry. I have a few things to do in Paris and in the south so maybe I will cut this visit short and await further news."

"Call me when you have a night for a meal, Dora is out but she said to arrange it." Joseph linked his arm with mine and we walked to the door.

"Absolutely, I am having lunch with Thierry now so I will call you later with some details. We'll definitely eat before I leave." I kissed him from cheek to cheek. "Thank you Joseph. It is such a blessed feeling knowing I have you taking care of the finances for us here in France. Thierry has really grown attached to you. I am forever grateful for the way you run my affairs."

"My love, really you are the easiest client I have. Half way across the world, trusting me over the phone. The pleasure absolutely is mine, you are like family to me."

"Thanks Joseph, I feel the same. I'll be in touch. Kiss kiss."

I walked down through his courtyard and out onto the Avenue Foch. The taxi rank was not far from his apartment. I wondered what I should do now? The renovation was still some time off and I'd left Annika with the restaurant preparations back home. I jumped in the taxi and offered the address for the restaurant for lunch, knowing I was going to have to tell Thierry that my stay would be more likely days than weeks.

"Bonjour Madame, your coat?" the maître de said as the valet opened the door for me.

"Merci Monsieur," I thanked him.

"Your guests have already arrived, please follow me."

The restaurant was full of business people, very efficient, very organised. Suits all round and I was glad I meshed in, not looking too touristy.

"Sass." Thierry stood up and pulled out my chair, giving me a kiss. Antoine also was there.

"Hi guys, wow, it's picking up some weather out there. Antoine, how are you? I'm glad you could make it." I gave him a big hug.

"I am great Sass, it's wonderful to see you. Thierry said you only arrived this morning? You have no doubt already been hard at work?" he enquired, concerned.

"I have Antoine, but that's what I'm here for so no need to worry. I had a great flight and the visit with our accountant has put me in a good frame of mind, so all is good. As you say, ces't bon'." I winked at him and he relaxed back in his chair. Thierry looked up at me when I mentioned Joseph.

"How is Joseph?" he enquired.

"Seems great, you know he's doing the London Marathon?" I asked.

"Mmm I do, not sure I approve, he's really going hard at it. Hope it's not a heart attack waiting to happen," he frowned.

"I think he is being very careful Thierry, he's not silly. He wouldn't do it if his doctors told him not to."

Thierry shrugged the way he does as if to say, "not overly happy about it but hey, not my life". I rubbed the sleeve of his shirt.

"He'll be fine honey, you know just because we're old doesn't mean we're fragile."

He left it hanging, hating it when I mentioned my age, me not at all concerned with it and loving to use it occasionally.

"Anyway," I said, "he says as he does every time we speak what an amazing job you are doing and how well everything is coming together. Both of you, so here's to Restaurant6."

A bottle of champagne arrived and we sat in silence, just enjoying the moment. The chef had prepared a special menu for us and the wine had been chosen to match. I leant back in my chair while the boys talked and looked around the room. Very busy, the staff and chefs were going fast. The flamingo light fittings dotted the ceilings and reflected the pink of their beaks in the mosaic tiles on the walls. The black and white cow-hide chairs were starting to look tired but the grey slate carpet and the huge luscious cream drapes hid some of the age. The staff here were all quite beautiful - one of Thierry's favourite things about the place - and they doted on the boys with little subtlety. Antoine was always keen to respond and provide some reaction but Thierry typically appeared either unimpressed or he did not notice. It's this attitude, I considered, that made him seem above his peers. He had always given others the perception that he could take or leave anyone or anything at a moment's notice. It's a detachedness that makes him come across as aloof but not off-guard. He was completely comfortable in his own skin and appeared to possess genuine confidence. There was no doubt that some of it was real but the rest he faked and faked extremely well. I knew it was his game and it was fine with me. He had years to make the rest of it come true. We discussed the progress of the renovation and, regretfully, how little I could do, at least for the time being.

"I was going to head down and see Christelle," I reminded him. "Maybe I'll go tomorrow, get it out of the way while everything is on track here. Did you say you were keen also, or is that going to throw you out?" I asked casually, Thierry not one to be organised for.

"I was keen," he replied. "How are you going?" he asked.

"TGV, it goes every hour. I'll get a car at the other end and drive to her place. Let me know, no pressure. I'll only stay a night or two."

"Yep, I'll see how I go," he said more to himself than to me.

Lunch passed with usual good laughs from Antoine, who was constantly getting in trouble on the streets and with his family, and Thierry and I relaxed into his company. As the wine flowed so did the stories and before long the chefs were knee-deep in outdoing each other for the worst stories. Antoine's girlfriend arrived, Dominique, and just like Antoine she slotted in seamlessly to the conversation.

Thierry and I headed outside for a smoke.

"It's good to see you Sass," he offered. "It's like having family around when you're here. I miss you when you go."

I hugged him around the waist. "I love it here. I love all the stories, the kitchen life, the restaurant life, you name it. It means everything to me to be a part of it. You are one of my dearest friends. Seeing you is like coming home." A tear fell down my cheek and I realised for the first time how much I missed being around him. We had been through so much together and to have this connection on the other side of the world always overwhelmed me. The fact that I could talk to him about Tom and the restaurant at home, was more than most got from their business partners - let alone chefs. I looked up at him and noticed a strange look pass over his face it. I caught my breath.

"Hey, the wine is settling in. Before you know it we'll be planning our next restaurant in, I don't know... Australia!" I joked. "You finished?" I asked, looking at his cigarette.

"Mmm," he nodded. "Do you know, I..." his sentence trailed off and he turned and looked down at me, my arm still around his waist.

"Do I know what?" I repeat.

"Ahh, do you know what time you'll go to Christelle's tomorrow?" he stammered.

"Leave around noon, I think. It's close to four hours, the train. Come back about the same time a day or two later. You don't have to come, honey. She'll understand." I squeezed him tight, not that there was much to squeeze.

"Yeah. Inside? It's cold."

The maître de opened the door for us and Antoine and Dominique were in hysterics, both of them doubled over, tears running down their cheeks.

"What on earth did we miss?" I laughed, appreciating the change of mood.

"Oh Sass," Dominique croaked, "You're going to love this one."

The afternoon rolled into the early evening and the early evening into the late. We ended up at my favourite bar in St Germain, and we shouted over the top of the music.

"Sass, you better book the TGV or you'll never get there," Thierry warned.

"Yep, you're right. Won't be a sec guys, just going upstairs where it's a bit quieter," I replied.

"Book two seats," he told me.

I gave him the thumbs up sign and headed upstairs. The staircase was one of my favourites. The iron of the balustrading was simple and quite thin, not at all like the heavy ironwork typical of France, and the treads were worn down timber pieces, each one separate and slightly different. Hanging down through the well was an oversized green plant, again very fine but long and fragile. Tiny candles flicked through the plants, delicate limbs lit every night by hand one by one. The wall behind the staircase was covered in only white books. From the first floor all the way up to the third floor. It was one huge bookcase and one huge amount of white books. Sometimes I came in the daytime just to stand on the staircase and work my way up through the layers of shelving and the impressive collection of books. It was the only white thing in the entire venue and the effect was stimulating. This was living in Paris: behind every corner, the very next step you took, a vision, a thought-provoking image. Maybe it wasn't living in Paris at all - maybe it was the visitor, the tourist that felt that way, but even so - expect nothing and look for everything. It was all here in Paris. Even the mere breath of the word, just the 'Pa' before you finished the 'ris' suggested uncertainty, mystery, intrigue, adventure. Nothing remained still in Paris. There was motion even on this old staircase, dust covering the bookshelves, there was motion. There was an old film playing on every book spine, it made you want to look closer to see if it was really there, to touch and feel it, possibly walk into it and be found right here in Paris. I loved this staircase, it was poetic.

When I got back downstairs the group were on tequila rounds and I realised that was my cue for departure; I had never fared well on tequila. I kissed all goodbye, gave Thierry the train details and grabbed a taxi. I passed the main tower and I saw it was midnight. "Ooh la la," I thought, "no wonder I was done." I hoped there was hot water running at the hotel or tomorrow would be a right struggle. I relaxed back into the taxi and watched the Paris lights fly by, head over heels again.

The next morning it was pouring down. I opened the luscious curtains of my favourite hotel room and decided instantly to change the car I booked last night for pick up in St Tropez. I knew all the cars, and roads for that matter in Europe were made for weather of any kind, but still I didn't want a buzz-box in a mad storm. I recall being intrigued when I first learnt that all the major roads and some smaller ones too were doused with salt to absorb the snow in the winter months, and that all the car's windscreen wipers had automatic sensors for the rainfall; the harder the fall, the faster they went. Still, knowing all this information never lessened my terror at driving in the rain in France. Because everyone else on the road was used to it they forgot about me dithering along, not used to it, and even though the speed limit was legally twenty kilometres less in the rain, very few seemed to adhere to it. I managed to get at least a Audi sedan instead of the buzz-box they had on hold for me.

"How's the weather in St Tropez?" I asked the Europcar receptionist.

"Wet, apparently," she said in her perfect 'what a stupid question' French.

As I hung up the phone breakfast arrived and I flicked on the TV looking for the only two satellite channels that spoke English; BBC and CNN. The new Pope was being inducted - or induced, both are applicable - and the channels had full coverage, both practically identical. He looked young, at least younger than any of the previous Popes who I guessed we only ever saw when they arrived at their deathbeds so perhaps the comparison was not really fair. Nonetheless, there was a lot riding on this young man, the faith in need of a real boost. Dipping my croissant into my coffee - a thing I only do when I'm in France or at home on the odd occasion when we have pastry for breakfast - I thought of the state the Catholics were in. Bad press every month, molestation, child abuse, adult abuse and the near-irrelevance religion had with generations Y and X. I wondered if like most other phases in the evolution of the world, this also would be a cyclic thing? Would the faith do a big U-turn and rebrand itself so that the youth viewed it more positively or as more relevant than it appeared at the moment? I remembered hearing an interview from the Archbishop of New England and the interviewer asked, "Has religion become irreligion?" I thought at the time, "that probably summarises it."

I rugged up in a thousand layers and called a concierge. A taxi was waiting to take me to the Gare de Lyon, a place of great energy that ignited me on every visit. I arrived half an hour early just to watch the comings and goings. I ordered an espresso and took a seat at Paul's Patisserie. It was almost lunchtime and the station was in full swing. The TGV was taking off and silently gliding in like sliding doors in a supermarket. People pulled their trolley bags along, hands gloved, earmuffs tight, collars up. They were brisk and on the move, with a purpose, a destination to get to. More than occasionally though there was the tourist; dazzled, confused, gathering deep breaths, preparing themselves for yet another foreign situation, to be confronted again after their safe train ride with chaos. They stared at monitors looking for a sign, something to give them a hint, a glimpse of where they were going or where they'd come from. Something appeared – Voila! A platform number! Bingo! - and they were off, shuffling furiously in one direction or another, dedicated to their itinerary, committed to their planning of months and months.

"Do you need another?" a voice asked me. It was Thierry.

"Ca va mon ami," I spoke, as usual. "You good?" I asked him.

"Oh, a bit, how do you say, 'rusty'? But I have the train. All will be good." He lit a cigarette.

"It looked dangerous when I left but hey, what the hell, just another night at the farm hey?"

He looked inquisitively at me.

"What is 'another night at the farm'?" he asked.

"Actually I'm not sure Thierry, I thought it was an expression we used, but now that you say it, it doesn't sound quite right. Maybe it's 'another day on the job'. I can't be sure. That has me quite puzzled. I was never good at colloquialisms. I'm sure there's something in it though, you know like 'when in Rome' or 'what's good for the goose' etc. Anyhow, glad you had a good night," I shrugged.

"I never said I had a good night," he responded. "Long, absolutely, good but not overly, more of the same." He put his cigarette out and finished his coffee.

"Oh honey, the joys of being a part of the scene. It gets easier as you get older you know. Make the most of it, one day you'll be married with kids and casually hanging out at bars will be a distant memory. Let's go, we've got five minutes before it leaves," I announced, grabbing my bag.

"I'm looking forward to marriage and kids. It's got to be better than gabbing at the bar," he said as we walked.

"Sure, but you've got your whole life for the former, might as well enjoy the latter whilst it's happening," I advised. "Bonjour Madame, seat 102 and 103," I informed the ticket collector.

"Oui Madame." Only slightly viewing our ticket she walked off down the platform. Sometimes you can travel on the TGV completely unknown to the universe. You walk up, get on, get to your stop, get off. This could take place over five or six hours, yet at other times it was like World War II and tickets were expected to be produced at the most random intervals. We found our carriage and our allocated seats and Thierry put our bags in the baggage storage. I'd booked seats with a table, they often had more room and I needed the table for my laptop. The train took off, Thierry was asleep within the minute and gladly I switched on my laptop, thankful for the quiet time. I perused my emails, opening them quickly, scouring through the content in search of anything that needed immediate attention then relaxed back into the task at hand. The carriage was fairly empty, two couples and a young female. She looked like a student, iPad in front of her, backpack to her side, laughing at something, Facebook. The two couples were older - not together though. One I think were speaking German, they certainly looked German. The other couple were English, the husband asleep and the wife fussing around with a lap-load of papers. Sitting back, my mind wandered to Tom. There was something so endearing about elderly couples travelling. It was a challenge at the best of times, least of all when you really didn't have to. Did they travel purely for the joy, the experience, the forgotten memories? Was it a bucket list? Finally enough finances to go? Whatever the reason, travelling with your long-term partner when you're elderly I assumed would be non-stressful. Each partner knew the other so well. There were no surprises, no over-expectations. Each person had their role and they played according to the rules, unlike when you were young. When you were young your expectations of your partner were purely a mirror of your own. If public transport was easy for you, so should it be for the other. If being carefree and casual was you then it was so for your partner. If five-star was for you then it must be for your partner. You were connected more by youth than by your actual relationship. You expected a twenty-five-year-old to behave like an average twenty-five-year-old. You didn't make allowances for idiosyncrasies, fetishes, personal whims or hang-ups, you were supposed to leave them all behind at the airport because you were young, you were independent and life was at its peak.

When Tom and I first starting traveling to France, he spoke the language and I organised the itinerary. He would suggest a handful of must-dos but the majority of it was as I wanted. He absorbed every detail, I absorbed every meal, drink, shop. Our first time together in Paris was our honeymoon. We fell in love with Paris, clichéd as it sounds, and declared it our preferred city (over the other three we had been to together). But the truth was I did love Paris, well before my honeymoon and luckily Tom felt it too. It was his first visit and it was Tom all over. Beautiful architecture, exquisite shops, old and wise, historical but relevant, food made for the Gods. I knew he would love it, the romantic in him could never have not. Later even, when we travelled further abroad we still returned home declaring our love for

Paris. We found ourselves comparing it to other cities we ventured to, when comparisons were near impossible.

I looked down at my hand and turned the ring around on my middle finger. He bought it for me in Lyon, our second favourite city in France, almost fifteen years ago. I had loved it every day, the yellow stone so subtle and unique. I glanced over at Thierry and smiled.

"Feeling better?" I enquired.

"Je suis bien. Are you ok?" he asked delicately. "You thinking about Tom?"

I looked more closely at him and smiled. "Gosh, do you know me that well! You'd think we were an old married couple," I joked with him.

He grinned at me. "No one would mistake me for your husband, you are far too elegant for such a gypsy."

"Yeah you're right, maybe more like my au pair or house cleaner. Actually, you'd do a great job of both. Sure chef-ing is your passion?"

"No, I only do it to be in business with you, so I can take all your money," he retaliated.

"Pfft, good luck with that! More like the other way around, superstar."

A red balloon randomly whipped past the window and it made me think of the village outside, a little girl or boy who just lost their balloon. Did they have another? Were they walking along with their mama holding hands, a day at the market, a birthday party? The sky outside had cleared, maybe it was their local supermarket handing out balloons for charity, mama needing to restock before the next downpour.

"I'm not half the superstar without Marie, you know," he laughed. "Thank god that's over. That was tiring business."

"Well you don't seem to be too short of company my love - only hearsay and what I read, of course. What is it they say, don't believe everything you read?"

I smiled happily, knowing that no life outside the restaurant could fade very fast. It was one thing to have Marie pressuring him not to work all the time, but just the same, to have nothing pressuring you not to work is not good either.

"You're right," he said in his serious manner. "You shouldn't believe all you read, but if it makes you happy," he shrugged.

I started to wonder if he could literally read my mind. He was still almost as mysterious to me as he was when we first worked together. Sure, I knew everything about him, his family, his life, but his thoughts and expressions somewhat eluded me. I knew his seriousness was not as serious at it seemed and he could joke at any moment, often taking me a second to realise it. I knew he had a heart of gold and was way too generous, and I knew he would fall on a sword for me, but could I read his mind? Not in a million years.

The train came to a halt and as if on cue the rain bucketed down outside the carriage.

"Right on cue, hey," Thierry commented back to the window, gathering our luggage.

"Right on cue," I echoed. "We're good whilst we're in the station but there's a good ten minute walk to Europcar," I reminded him.

"You wait here," he advised as we meandered through the train station towards the exit, "I'll get the car and pick you up, just out front."

"Thanks love, but I have to show ID and sign the forms. You wait here, I'll be fifteen tops."

I searched for the sign and saw it overhead, making my way in that direction.

"I'm coming, rain's not a problem," he said simply as we dashed out into it.

The rain was really bashing down on us in the small car, having not had my request for a larger car relayed and apparently the tiny Citroen was the only car left in the yard. Under the weather conditions I was not prepared to hustle my way to another hire-car company to no doubt face the same problem. Thierry entered the details of Christelle's address into the GPS while I searched for the radio station that runs constantly in France, twenty four hours a day. The GPS showed about a forty-five-minute drive from our current destination so we headed out of the parking lot and into the main town. It had grown quite dark outside with the heavy storm and I said a silent prayer to get us there safely.

"Is Christelle enjoying her new house?" Thierry enquired as he was looking out the side of his window at the town around us.

"I think she's honestly loving it, Thierry," I replied. "They have the nursery already for the baby and Thomas is only fifteen minutes away at work. Her dad helped her restore it a bit. I think they put in all new floorboards, did a full paint job and even knocked out some walls to open it up a little. She said she's being having a ball in the yard, planting trees and flowers I can't even say the names of."

He smiled. "Gardening not being one of your strong points, Sass, that doesn't surprise me."

"Mmm, I never did get the gardening bug. I know you love it, but admit it, that's mainly to please your mother since she's so fantastic at it. If she didn't have that amazing garden and be so passionate about it, you wouldn't either."

"Hey that's not true!" He pretended to be hurt.

"I had a green finger a long time before Mama inducted me. I was always rattling off to my girlfriend's plants and flower names whenever we strolled around the parks of Paris."

"Pfft," I scoffed, laughing. "When on earth did you stroll around the parks of Paris with or without girlfriends? Liar. Don't you mean the pubs of Paris? And it's a green thumb, arsehole, not green finger!" I could hardly contain myself as Thierry sat there trying to look indignant.

"I said green thumb, what's green finger? You're hearing things in your old age," he retorted, trying to be upset.

"Yeah, 'green finger, what is that' - maybe a French saying. Anyway, you're a tool and you know it. Shhh, there's something on the radio about the main road we're about to turn on to."

We listened carefully to the announcement; there had been an accident three kilometres up from where we were about to emerge and all traffic was being diverted about another mile on to go through St Emillie instead. I quickly re-entered details into the GPS, looking for an alternate route, knowing how congested the official one was going to be. The GPS redirected us and we headed across the highway off to the other side and through a roundabout in the direction of Hyere, where we were supposedly headed to.

"These little machines are amazing," Thierry exclaimed. "In no less than three seconds the satellite has picked up all these tiny roads from millions of miles away. It's really clever."

I agreed with him, confident in the GPS, using it without fail whenever driving around France. "The way it quickly changes your route when you take the wrong road is what constantly stuns me. Just one small left instead of a right and in the heartbeat it tells you where to take the next turn to get back on track."

He nodded in agreement. We travelled along in silence for a while, me focusing hard on driving through the torrential rain. It was getting into the early evening and outside it was almost pitch black. Finally I saw on the GPS we were only roughly ten minutes away from our destination. I didn't say anything to Thierry but looking around it felt like we were in the middle of nowhere. There were no signs anywhere and the roads had become single lanes and in pretty bad shape. We were bumping all over the place as the winds knocked the little car about and there was not a single light as far as the eye could see. I was leaning hard over the steering wheel, trying to get as much vision as possible for where I was driving. I saw up on the left a sign to 'Le Plage', feeling relieved knowing that Christelle's new home was by the sea. I leant back in my seat a little. The GPS was instructing the next left then right at the next roundabout. By the time I had taken the left the ocean was sprawled out in front of us and the road was in such bad shape that Thierry was holding on to the handle above as we got thrown around the road. I looked back at the GPS which appeared to be telling me to drive straight for the water. It was so dark, lights nowhere to be seen that I assumed there must be roads ahead that I just couldn't see.

"Thierry," I yelled over the din of the rain crashing onto the car, "do you think this is right? The GPS says go further another 200 yards then turn left. It looks like a dead end, don't you think? Isn't that the ocean just there?"

No sooner than I'd spoken a huge wave crashed just in front of us and I screeched on the brakes, sending us skidding to the left.

"Holy shit, that is the fucking ocean! This is a dead end, where the fuck are we?" I turned to him. "Are you alright?"

"Yep, yep I'm fine, you?" he screamed back.

"Fuck, hold on, I have to get us out of here."

Turning the inside car lights on I could just make out a massive choppy ocean right at the windscreen. "Fuck, I can't make out if the water is all around us or if that's road?"

Thierry jumped out and covered his head with his hands. Another wave landed at his feet and he jumped back, covered from the waist down.

"Get back in," I screamed, pushing the window down. "God Thierry, what the hell are you doing!"

Frantic, I kept yelling, but the wind and rain were taking my words out to sea.

"Thierry!" I screamed, leaning out his door, now drenched alongside the entire inside of the car. "Thierry!"

He turned back to me, only feet away, and jumped back in. "Shit Sass, you're soaked! What were you thinking!" he yells, trying to close the door of the car against the strong winds.

"What I was thinking?" I yelled at him, furious. "I thought the fucking ocean was going to take you, what the fuck where you thinking! I was screaming at you and then that wave came, I thought you were... I don't know what I thought."

"Ok ok, sorry, sorry," he said, holding my face. "I couldn't hear. I was checking the road to see where it started and finished. It's ok, I'm ok. You're not going to lose me, I'm sorry, I didn't mean to scare you. You ok, are you ok Sass?" he repeated softly to me, still holding my face.

I could hardly hear him, the noise outside deafening, but knowing in an instant I absolutely couldn't bear losing him too. Tears fell down my face and he gently wiped them with his thumb.

"It's ok baby, it's ok." I could feel his breath on my skin, my hands flew up to cover his, still cradling my face.

"I'm ok," I managed, letting out a deep breath. "Sorry."

"You scared me."

I pulled my hands away from his and leant back. "I'm sorry, I didn't mean to yell at you like that." I took another deep breath, my hands at my throat.

"I'm sorry Sass, I didn't hear you calling me." He moved his hands to my shoulders, his body leaning over his seat, concern flooding his face. Confused, I flinched at the touch and struggled to

128

recompose myself. A massive crack startled us both and we jumped, turning to look ahead.

"Shit Thierry, we've got to get out of here."

Shaking my head I reversed the car and pushed down on the pedal. Something was bogging us down and the back wheel spun furiously, going nowhere. I put the car into forward, trying to move off the spot and it lurched forward like it was dipping us into the unknown. I tried again to reverse, not knowing which direction was which, outside was pitch black and the rain was a huge curtain. The car reversed, I gripped the wheel and pushed down hard on the accelerator. I could feel the ground firm up under the car and quickly spun it around to get out of there. We drove for about five minutes before I saw the light of a closed hotel and I pulled over under the glow. Dripping wet, I looked at Thierry; he was staring straight ahead.

"Thierry, I'm so sorry. Are you ok?"

"I'm sorry Sass, I don't know what's come over me, I... I... don't know what came over me," he mumbled, still staring straight ahead. "But yep, I'm ok."

I looked at the GPS and wondered whether I could trust it to get us out of here. Reading my mind, he said "We have no other option. Maybe the storm interfered with the satellite, I don't know."

I typed in Christelle's details and it gave us a 10-minute drive.

"You're drenched Thierry. Should we look for a hotel around here or try and make it to Christelle's?" I asked.

"I don't think we're going to find much around here. This place is deserted - obviously the storm is bad for business."

I agreed and I turned the car back on. There was no reception on my phone which made me concerned for the GPS instructions.

"Do you have reception? " I enquired.

"Nope, so I hope that the GPS knows what it's doing the second time around," he echoed my thoughts.

I drove slowly, concentrating on the road and the storm, not wanting to end up on another ocean-view drive. The roads were seriously deserted and I could not fathom why there were absolutely no lights anywhere. I asked Thierry.

"Maybe the power is out," he offered. I supposed that could be it, which if it was, was not going to be so great at Christelle's. The GPS eloquently informed us that we had reached our destination and I pulled over, relieved at the sight of a house in front of us. I couldn't make out the number on the wall but I didn't care, it had to be somewhere close.

"Wait here," I told Thierry, "I'll go and check."

"No Sass, you're not going anywhere without me. You have no idea whose house this is. You wait here and I'll go. I'm already wet and fierce-looking. If it's trouble they won't want to mess with me," he smirked at me.

"Thierry," I smiled. "Do as you want."

Exhausted, I leant back in my seat and he opened his door.

"Sass, I'll be back. You are stuck with me for the rest of your life. I, I... I'll be back ok." With that he shut the door and made a run for the intercom. I watched him through the rain, keeping my eyes on his back. What was I feeling? He came back to the car and closed his door.

"No one's home," he said. "But I want you so badly Sass, I can't stop myself. I want to do it here in the car, later in a hotel, after that in my bed and after that wherever but forever."

He pulled open my shirt and his hands went to my breasts. A light came on by the gate, I looked away from him and pulled myself up. I could just make out Thomas's face and I pushed Thierry back, relieved.

"It's them, look! Oh yeah, and they must have electricity," I announced shrilly.

"Sass," he whispered.

"Sorry Thierry, I don't know what happened. It's this storm, it was the thought of losing you - but you're like my brother, we were scared but it's ok now, they're home, tomorrow will be a new day and we can pretend that this never happened."

Looking away I gathered up my things; my phone, my bag, his cigarettes. "Come on," I said, " Thomas is waving at us!" I jumped out of the car and raced towards him, embracing him firmly. "Thomas, what is this storm? We got lost and almost ended up in the ocean!" I exclaimed, sounding far more joyous than I actually was.

"Oh Sass, it's crazy. We have been so worried. Your cell didn't have reception," he explained.

Thierry arrived and they hugged happily.

"I didn't know Thierry was travelling with you? What a relief, we thought you were on your own." He moved us down the covered path to the house. "Christelle will be so happy to see you Thierry, what a superb surprise!"

In true Thierry style he threw his arm around Thomas's shoulder, genuinely happy to see him. "Mate," he said, "the surprise has all been mine," and he winked at me as we went through into the house.

I laughed aloud. "Next time, we'll fly the whole way!" I grinned, knowing that whatever had happened had been packed up, stored in a suitcase and sent first class to an unknown island somewhere out of our reach. Thierry put his other arm around me.

"As long as there is a next time, as long as we're all still together." He rushed off to Christelle with another wink.

Concealing my happiness and embarrassment, I linked arms with Thomas as I saw a very pregnant Christelle coming down from the hallway.

The rest of the trip went by with very little interruption. As usual there was too much eating and drinking and not enough of anything else. I shopped for the kids and Annika and picked up some great items for the fit-out at home, and doubled up on some of the more loose objects that would work in both restaurant venues.

For my return home, Thierry insisted on driving me to the airport and arranged to pick me up at six from my hotel.

"Got everything?" he asked as he loaded the gear into his car.

"Yep, all is good. Ready to go," I replied, jumping into the front seat.

"The restoration is supposedly a month away but I'm sure that's going to be more like two, given how it's gone so far. It's up to you when you come back. We've agreed we won't do a gala night so we'll do something small whenever you get here."

"Yeah it's going to be a hard one to plan for. I guess we'll just play it by ear. I'm not necessary for any of it, just moral support and to give you a hand. The show goes on much better without me, so maybe we'll call it a trip in six months and go from there. Then there's no pressure," I shrugged, knowing my involvement was absolutely useless. Sure I could comment on fit-out and bits and pieces but I didn't need to be in Paris to do that.

"Don't stay away six months. It'll be old hat by then, you'll have to see it in its glory. Come back in September, bring Annika, the kids, whatever," he said firmly.

"Honey, the kids are not at all interested in travelling over here. Sure they were up for it when Tom was alive, but it's my dream, not theirs. They would rather be with Grandma and Pop, you know that," I apologised.

"Sure, but if it gets you here quicker and longer," he said casually.

"Are you ok, Thierry?" I was now getting concerned.

"Oui oui, I'm absolutely fine. No problem, but it's nice having you here to bounce the business off. It all just seems more worth it when you're here, it all makes more sense. Ah, it's no big deal, three months, six months, what's the difference." He banged his hand on the steering wheel, angry.

"Thierry, why don't you come back for a week or two while they finish the renovation? Antoine is good, you have Stephane working out. Carrie can hold the fort. Just clear your head, have a break before it seriously peaks with the new dining room. The weather at home is beautiful at the moment and the kids would love to see you. Take Andrea and Sebastian to the beach for a couple of days, they're working hard too and could use some time off. What do you say? It's a great idea!" I exclaimed enthusiastically, also sad to be saying goodbye.

"I don't know," he looked at me. "There's still a shitload to do and they all make bullshit if I'm not around to supervise."

"But you said yourself, it's just up to the builders now. All the contracts are done and the architect seems to be there as much as you," I argued, happy to have seen him there nearly every day as I arrived.

"Ok, I'll give it some thought. The ocean is definitely calling me now that you mention it. I'll give it some thought," he smiled at me.

"Great, but promise me you will book a flight when you get home, then it's done," I demanded.

"Righto, you got the point across, now travel safe. Either way we have a restaurant that needs both of us, in whatever country we are in," he laughed.

"Bye honey, you know I love you. I miss you already." Tears were pricking my eyes and I hugged him tight.

"See you Sass," he simply said. "Take care, you are precious."

I blew him a kiss and he blew one back. He raised his eyebrows and smiled, I smiled broadly. What a team.

Chapter Three

The rain was pouring down, wind sweeping palm fronds back and forth, windows almost impossible to see out of. I hadn't really thought it would happen, I realised, standing in the entrance of the new restaurant, looking out though the arch windows to the slightly visible pavers of the street below, the view of the city peering in through rain, the charm of the glass panelling even more intensified by the weather knocking it around. Looking at my watch I saw there was another hour before she was due. My left shoe was hurting like hell. I kicked it off and rubbed my foot up the back of my calf. I squeezed my toes together, trying to dull the pain and put my foot back in the shoe. I might as well head back to the cafe downstairs and grab a coffee, kick my shoes off for a while and wait for her there. The place was deserted and the furniture out on the footpath was getting a battering from the storm.

I stood at the counter. A waitress called out "Hi there, won't be a moment. The kitchen is closed sorry, you know with this weather we haven't had anyone come in in hours so the chefs have gone home. Do you still want something?"

I looked at the waitress and thought to myself again, how hard is it? Why give me the negative spiel as the introduction? The only way to start a conversation with a potential diner was with positivity, how else were you going to get their money? I offered rather sheepishly, "I was interested in a coffee but I am waiting for a friend who's still another hour away yet. Are you trying to close up? It's only a coffee so no big deal."

"Nah we stay open through to dinner but, like I said, the kitchen is closed and I've got some work to do. So you can stay here but there's not much doin'."

"Great," I replied with a huge smile. "That would be fantastic, if I could take a long black you won't hear boo from me again, probably stick your head up at some stage and I'll be gone, thanks heaps. I am in real need of some caffeine."

She smiled at me and grabbed the handle of the coffee machine, grinding the coffee at the same time. I wandered around the small room looking for a comfy spot, somewhere not in the way of the girl but dry enough too. As I was wandering I noticed the place was actually quite quaint. It was the first time I'd really been in and sat down. It was in need of some TLC and the menu read fairly blandly, but the fit-out was interesting enough and the seats were a good fit. The waitress arrived with my coffee and some water.

"Make yourself at home, don't think anyone's going to be interrupting you anytime soon," the waitress explained.

Smiling, I thanked her and opened up my laptop. Clicking on my 'concepts' file I opened up the drawings the drafter had sent me and start to make notes, thoroughly absorbed, head down.

I thought of Annika. I was so happy for her, concerned also, that maybe somewhere along the way she may have decided it was a mistake to stay where she was in her idyllic lifestyle back on the island. Over the years we had grown close. Six years later since we first met; the mutual love of food, the sadness in our history and being alone had cemented our relationship. We also enjoyed the same kinds of books, often disliked the other's choice in movies and both subscribed to the 'Populous', a newspaper only available online and about global issues. My children loved her, my husband's family loved her, my family loved her - even my mother. I remembered a note from my mother lying on the kitchen bench, about shoes and socks being left at her place, if I needed them they were on the back porch. With the loss of Tom mum had softened, cried and sobbed. It shook her out of her postage stamp existence. She showed a side of her I had only witnessed once before and even then it was so long ago that I was not sure if the memory was real or not. She was tender and caring, kind and compassionate. After the accident mum brought out photos of Tom and put them around her house, she spoke to my children of him often and sometimes I would catch her with an absent, faraway look in her eyes and when she would turn to talk to me, to respond, there would be mist on her cheeks, the spell broken. She asked me frequently how I was doing, not judging like she used to, ready to advise, complaining about how I was handling this or that. Now whatever I did or didn't do she found perfectly acceptable. I knew I was hard, complicated and distant; the bucket list, learning the guitar, random travels, random sobbing. She accepted this and stood close, she shielded the children when needed from passing conversations or visiting mourners. Mum had been exactly what I needed and it was only later, after some of the dark had passed, like when I watched the clouds move along the moon at nightfall, that it dawned on me that she had been grieving too. Maybe she was only grieving the memory of the grief that had consumed her when her husband died, something that none of us had ever quite acknowledged. In my parent's separation I had been too consumed with myself and, sad to say it now, but, him. The disappointment, hurt and heartache was potentially worse than death, no closure, no evidence of moving on, scared and frightened of what still might come, the long years ahead still frequenting the same haunts. Thinking about Tom, my feelings got more complicated. The anger had lessened and I had tucked the grief away in a small part of my heart but the loss remained and the loneliness sat on my shoulder, like a parrot constantly screeching words at me that no one else could hear.

It had been a long time since I let my mind wander to the luggage, still unopened up in the attic, gathering dust. My sister and my best friend never mentioned it again after I confided in them. The police just dumping them the suitcases with no authentic explanation, an oversight on behalf of the investigation that the contents of the boot of the car had not been returned. Five months and eight days later they realised, five months and nine days later they returned them. Discarded them, rather, more like a nuisance, like they must have been clearing out someone's old home or old storage unit and found them. My husband's suitcases from his car that overturned from a head-on collision with a truck travelling too fast, near an idyllic beachside village. That was what killed him.

I looked up and the rain had stopped, Annika was walking casually along the pretty paved street. A small smile lined her face and her ponytail swung back and forth like a schoolgirl's. Instantly the thoughts of Tom and his secret unopened luggage were pushed away and I waved excitedly at her. Seeing me, her face broke into a broad smile and she quickened her pace.

"Hey honey, you look very relaxed sitting there. All things going to plan for once?"

"Hi love, mmm so-so. But you look refreshed, come from the pool?"

"Yep, so a coffee would be a treat."

"Don't get too excited, I think the waitress has gone into hiding. I'm the only one who's been here all afternoon - apparently the bad weather has kept everyone away. She was pretty keen to disappear."

"I'll have a sticky beak. If I track her down, another?"

"No thanks love."

Typical of Annika, I thought, no fuss, no agitation, if the waitress was nowhere to be seen Annika would simply go without, no problem, end of story. She came back five minutes later.

"Well if she was here, she's MIA now. Let's get going, you've paid?"

Honesty was an imperative with her. Not the kind of open book honesty, "Hi, how are you, here's my life story" or "Here's what I really think of you", but the moral honesty, the values placed upon doing right by all, all the time. The belief that if the universe was so then there must be something much larger at play, and if this was so, the laws that were introduced at the beginning of time should be highly regarded and completely abided by. There was no faltering. It was a domino effect, it was quantum physics. If all things were equal - which she firmly believed they were - then no one had any options anyway. Destiny was still one's own fate, achievable, contemplated, slightly recognisable when it arrived but still a matrix, still part of a bigger and much more complex plan that depending on the rules you followed determined which part of the matrix you might be destined to inhabit.

By the time I gathered up my make shift work station and vetted a call from a supplier who had let me down continuously since we started organising the new business, the waitress had reappeared.

"Thanks for coming ladies, see you next time."

We looked at each other, slightly confused, slightly bemused.

"Is the coffee machine still on for a takeaway by any chance?" Annika asked sweetly, seeming to be completely sympathetic to her situation.

"Um well let me see, ah yeah that should be ok for a takeaway," the waitress fumbled then relented.

I knew if that had been me asking, no way. Annika had a way of making people do what she needed them to do.

As we ascended to the first floor the sound of the rain vanished and stepping out into the room of the restaurant, brilliant blue skies greeted us.

As always, when I first entered this space I found myself holding my breath. There was an energy that oozed from the atmosphere outside, filled up all the windows around the room until they could no longer hold it out and it burst in, in microscopic rays of shimmering silver and white hues dancing around the ceiling, pirouetting up the walls and finally lazing back on sunbeds on the floor, arms crossed behind their heads, drinking up the giddiness. I was in love with it from the moment I walked in.

Looking around the room again I mentally visualised all the walks of life that would inhabit it. The many guests who would come here for so many different reasons. I'd watch them , serve them, learn from them and in return they would walk away happy and content within themselves. Chuffed to be one of the lucky ones who came to dine here. They would pat themselves on the backs for being so educated, so knowledgeable, affluent enough to attend not only here, but restaurant after restaurant like this. They would steel themselves for the right conversation breaker with their colleagues at work, their peers of superiority or friends of lesser status to introduce the activities of their weekend. Change the topic subtly, then barrage their audience with tiny details of the dining experience. Maybe their audience was as sophisticated as they perceived themselves and they could contribute even, compare and swap experiences, ooh and ahh over the luscious descriptions on the menu and make a mental note to attend at the very next possible opportunity. Their status would define them as cultural, worldly, informed. I recognised the irony of my situation, accepting the fact that I had swapped airports for restaurants, arrival lounges for cocktail lounges, coffee stools for bar stools and yet here, twenty years on, nothing changed, people didn't change. People were people; generally uninspiring, generally willing to settle. What made people opt out of life? Where did they learn that it was appropriate to be underwhelmed? Acceptable to be overlooked? I looked into their eyes and mostly they lacked sparkle, a fire, determination and then sometimes if I looked hard enough I saw a silence that was screaming loudly, "This is not me! Please don't think this is me! I am trapped in here, help!" Then there were moments when I felt the customer before I saw them. Their presence arrived first, like the suggestion of rain when it was imminent, the smell of grass heightened and you looked to the sky for confirmation. Sadly, they were of course the exceptions. Often the world had moved on without them. Yet they existed, with absolute certainty they existed. Life was there and ready to take. You could compare it to shopping in the supermarket as you walk up and down the aisles of a clinically refined, hyper analysed supermarket, fluorescent lights overhead, refrigerators quietly buzzing, tiles shiny clean. Each aisle showcased the magnitude of opportunities you could buy. Grab the items you need, pop them in your trolley, nod to the other customers shopping alongside you and head to the checkout. "That will be twenty years," says the checkout chick, no problem. You pay with some wrinkles, some excess weight. An amount of money must be exchanged, sure, but that's beside the point. You offer up half your identity for roughly half the years you may have left before you finalise the transaction and throw in a handful of energy and esteem hoping you might get it back next time you come to shop. Done, start the unpacking and should you come across something you're unsure why you bought, take it back, exchange it and use that instead. Simple. But people were inclined to think the supermarket should do the shopping for them. Dump the trolley at the checkout and be satisfied with the contents within. We were losing all ability to think freely, for ourselves, originally, to have original thought. We were becoming governed by what our neighbours thought, our colleagues thought, by what the new friends we meet thought.

Standing in front of the window I looked down to where a table and two chairs would sit. On instinct I touched the back of the imaginary chair, connected with the customer. I was there, I could meet their every need. I would catch the glimpse, the sideways look, the vacancy, the defeat. The process would be routine, familiar. It would confirm life is as it was. But then someone would turn up, would appear at the door and I would know they had arrived. It would me make giddy with relief, happy and joyous. It would reconnect, reconfirm what I knew was possible, was achievable, was a must for life. They would affirm all that I believed in, simply by the way they arrived into my lounge room at the restaurant.

Annika fell in love with the space and the concepts too. We discussed variations, agreed on more seating, the cold room needed expanding to probably double. We looked through the drawings week after week, moving the one table and chair we had around, confirming the best aspects for the guests. The bar was broadened, seating capacity increased and toilets resituated. We decided on delicate stained glass pendants for the large arched windows and heavier warmer pendants for the bar. The ceiling remained completely mirrored, mirroring the windows, birds and butterflies, creating an effect that brought the sky into the room. There had been lengthy discussions with Annika as my new business partner, about how far we should go on our own and we concluded that we would attempt it together, enjoy the process and make it a part of the journey. I was confident that we could do it, having had significant involvement in all previous ventures. I was also quietly thrilled to be working with a girlfriend for the first time. Not that working with my husband, or builders or chefs had been terrible - far from it - but the relationship that girlfriends have is special and very different. There just seemed to be a connection, a parallel. She would finish my sentence, arrive with a picture of exactly what we needed. I would drag her around the antiques stores and we would see it simultaneously together. No need to even speak, the ticket taken from the object ready to be paid at the counter. We would toss and turn in our own minds the uncertainty of a particular issue until we finally put it on the table, only to realise the other had been going through the same agony. It was a partnership in the true sense of the word, authentic and genuine. It had been a taskforce on all the restaurants before and over time I had picked up on techniques and ideas, listening to the experts at play probably in the hope that eventually I could enjoy the experience, that Annika and I could have fun with it and make it ours.

As we sat in the builder's office looking through the first concepts and outlines of the rough draft we had given him, the feeling overwhelmed me. It was ours, on paper, in front of us. Just Annika and me, two girls from nowhere special, pain and suffering under our belt, betrayal and hurt a part of what brought us together. Yet above and beyond any of that was the love of living. The dedication to survival, and not just survival but thriving survival. Our optimism was our founding bond, our sense of adventure and excitement kept us together. When Annika had suggested we do it together with a real foundation and a genuine partnership, I thought "why not?". She was full of surprises, her project management skills were exceptional, her police force training went clearly far ahead of drills and physical strength. Her communication and negotiating techniques were worthy of a career far beyond cooking, and she loved what she did. I had never seen her so alive. The builder she chose was a bit of a shark and they had gotten off to a rocky start, but now she had him eating out of her palm. I knew her beauty sweetened the deal but it was really about her capabilities. She spent night after night reading or on the internet, learning about the build. He started to speak to her like a student or an apprentice, explaining the various jobs that the boys were doing and she would listen intently until he was finished, then humbly summarise it with full comprehension. He gradually learnt that what she didn't know she would find out, and that she understood better probably than most builders he knew.

It was fair to say we had misjudged Ian. We hired him for his excellent referrals. It was unquestionably remarkable craftsmanship. He was also within our budget, which wasn't lean but was all we were prepared to pay. Moreover he appeared to be not too challenged by the prospect of working with two women.

The first builder we went to see was from an era not of our time. We were ushered in by a very attractive young blonde female, the foyer as impressive as her. She had huge round eyes, with long lashes, a tiny waist and perfect blonde shoulder-length hair. She sat, in a pair of tight leggings and vintage-looking boots. Her dimples were infectious when she smiled at us; upon welcoming us we had no alternative but to bag the biggest possible smile and hold it for as long as we could. It was disconcerting, I lost all perspective as to why we were there, so consumed with this girl's dimples. I looked across at Annika who also was smiling like someone had just announced she had won lotto. What was making us do this strange thing with our mouths? No matter what logical thoughts were going through my brain, I couldn't shake the smile. Every word she spoke included her dimples. She smiled even as she said words like 'won't' and 'take' and 'next'. These words were hard to say in performance smiles but there she was. Annika moved away and took a seat - I followed her lead, not knowing what had been discussed.

"Ok can I stop smiling now?" I asked Annika, exhausted.

"Yep," she let out a sigh. "Wow, that was intense. How does someone retain that smile all day long? Do you think she smiles even when no one is here to see her?"

"Well I guess the builder is here to see her. Is that unkind?" We let it drift off into a smile-sphere somewhere and waited patiently for Stephen T. Scott to see us.

He appeared moments later at his oversized double timber doors, much older than I had expected. Nearing his 70s, I guessed, he was well-spoken and well-dressed.

"Ladies," he said, "when your husband or husbands arrive please let Beth know and we can begin."

Quickly Annika stood, extending her hand. "Hi Mr Scott, pleasure to meet you. I'm Annika and this is Sass. Maybe I didn't explain myself to – Beth, is it? - but there are no husbands so we are ready."

I stayed seated, swinging my crossed leg, quite bemused by the whole situation and still wondering if I was going to break into smile again should Beth become involved.

"Ahh," he said, a little mystified. "Beth, have you got the file?"

Annika very politely looked from him to her. "Sorry Mr Scott, but it's somewhat irrelevant what the 'file' says. There is now, and only ever will be, Sass and myself for this project. Is that an issue for you?" She spoke now with genuine interest, disbelief underlying the final point.

"Well, ahh, Annika, it's certainly not how I got to where I am, isn't that right Beth? My wife has stayed at home and raised our four beautiful children with resounding success, having the time of her life along the way. She has more friends than I can poke a stick at, she does yoga, tennis and aqua aerobics weekly and takes frequent - and I will say probably a bit too frequent - shopping trips down south, while I work, giving her the existence she loves. I don't interfere with her job and she doesn't interfere with my job. Men are by nature the best breed for providing, for making money, for making accurate and astute decisions. Now I don't know where your husbands are today, and since I'm rarely wrong in my impressions of people I would undoubtedly guess that women as beautiful as yourselves are married, and that somehow your husbands have been tricked into letting you into whatever farcical ideas you may have." He closed his door and walked towards us. "Why don't you give Beth their numbers and I will on your behalf have a chat with them, and we'll see what this little project's all about. I'm sure I can probably convince the men to allow you to be involved on some level, if that's going to keep the peace."

Holding Annika's elbow, he looked over at Beth who immediately began her smiling routine. Within a second my face broke into a marathon smile and I looked to Annika for hope. Sure enough, she too was smiling like a Cheshire cat. Robotically, under some blonde smile spell, we wrote down mobile numbers for Beth's dimples and walked back out of the room, closing another pair of huge oversized timber doors behind us. I wanted to run back in and return to my normal self but I was immobilised. I wondered what the two of them were doing now. Was she down on all fours panting, her leggings hanging loosely around her boots while big daddy bent over her and thrust his oversized penis up her undersized ass? Was he grabbing at her crotch, riding her, laughing at us while she smiled happily, content with 'this is the way it should be'? My imagination was running wild as we realised that they had to be related, their appearances so similar it was obvious. I spun back around and made for the steps up to the doors, barging them open, convinced I would catch the creep being creepy. Before Beth even had a chance to look up from behind her desk where she was sitting quietly I turned and ran We drove home half laughing, half squirming.

Chapter Four

"What do you mean?" she asked Jack, her newest recruit.

"Well, I'm just not sure if he said he needed your services or if he already engaged your services."

"Did he have a name, Jack?" she asked slowly.

"Oh, I'm sure he does, but he spoke so quickly I couldn't tell if he mentioned it. He was either in the biggest hurry or he was bored with having to explain himself, but either way what I told you was all I could pick up." Shrugging his shoulders, he felt like he did well enough given the situation.

"OK, stay with me Jack - so all he said was to tell Audrey to meet him at 3pm at the Provence building in town today? That's about it?"

"As I already said, Audrey. I assumed you must have known him so I said ok. He murmured that he needed you for something or had already engaged you to do something so he'd see you there."

"And Jack, no name, no number?"

"Well no, as I said I just figured you were expecting it, the call that is. Sorry Aud, but can I go now? You know where to meet him." And with that he was back on the phone.

She looked at him, wondering how could she have hired someone so useless. She couldn't deny that he was a delight to have around and the clients seemed to really connect with him, but as for details he was terribly bad - which was a huge issue for a design company. She looked through her computer's database searching for a client that might fit the bill. She couldn't rule any of her male clients out considering he didn't say who he was. Sometimes they needed her for some of the strangest reasons. She also couldn't assume it was an existing client, however strange a manner for someone wanting to engage her to act. Surely they would be far more informative than that. Her mind wandered back to Jack laughing loudly down the phone and the anger started to bubble in her. "I'm sure he doesn't miss any details his friends feed him," she thought. "How bloody hard is it? In Korea this wouldn't happen, staff are thorough." At the thought of Korea her mind drifted to her previous life. The one where she had a successful job, not that this one wasn't but she was no way near as advanced in her career now that she was back at home that she had been in Korea. Not to mention her fiancé, their friends, their lavish lifestyle and his impending success, they great fortune Shane had amassed during their relationship. What irony that was. Jack laughed again, she resolved to taking him off the phones or at the very least she would have to streamline his position, work out exactly what he brought to the table and leave it at that. She grabbed her bag and an empty file pad. Either way she couldn't afford not to show. She headed outside and hailed a taxi.

Paying the fare she headed across to Provence Building, one of the oldest ones in the city. She instructed the driver to drop her off a little before so she could get her bearings and suss the place out. She knew the building had recently been refurbished, and standing on the corner street below it she was in awe of the job they had done. She tried to recall what she read about the refurbishment, the architects had done a perfect job in keeping its character and yet injecting some contemporary aspects at the same time. It was always an impressive building, photography schools always used it for its characteristics and if she thought back now, it was something like the most photographed building of the town, in the city. Wedding parties came in droves to have their moment captured down the side of the entrance. The brickwork and iron architecture were unique to the city. Now it looked even more grand, more European and, she thought, more flocked with sightseers and amateur photographers.

She looked around at the couple of surrounding cafes for a familiar face but recognised no one. The streets were relatively quiet - not end of work yet, and past the lunch hour. A man in a business suit appeared from a door alongside the cafe in the building and looked straight at her. She raised her eyes to him but he kept on walking. Considering her next plan of attack, she decided that rather than wander around looking suspicious with the chance of having the cops arrive, alerted by one of the waiters at the cafes, she would casually lean against the entrance for approximately ten minutes then leave. She didn't like surprises and didn't like being caught unawares. She was always in control. Even when her situation in Korea became sticky and she thought she was going to lose everything, she never lost her control. Her father at least taught her that. She turned to one side and saw a nice-looking man looking as uncertain as her. He was tanned and willowy. Pink checked shirtsleeves rolled up to his elbows, dark blue no-fuss pants and tan thongs. He was perhaps in his forties and had kind eyes. He nodded to her and offered his hand, a huge diver's watch on his wrist.

"Audrey Agencies?" he enquired.

"Yes," she replied thankfully, "Audrey," she said shaking his hand.

"Thank you for coming, agreeing to meet with me on such short notice. Ian, a pleasure to meet you."

She had a good feeling about him. He seemed not at all like some of the clients she had. Architecture could be often treated with an air of mystique and clients were either suspicious, untrusting or basically not sold on the profession as a whole. Alternatively, they critiqued and over-analysed, giving suggestions here and there and regarding themselves as somewhat of a Phillipe Stark. This guy seemed a little too normal, a straight-shooter. She knew instinctively that he was not in design, probably a project manager or a builder himself.

"I take it you're interested in some design work, unless you're here on behalf of one of my existing clients?" she asked, trying to get to the bottom of this meeting.

"Ah yes," he answered, a little unsteady. "I'm not so great with words, it might be better if I show you rather than explain it to you. Would you be comfortable with that?"

She nodded. It was daytime and the cafes were right here if she needed somewhere to run or scream. She couldn't deny he had piqued her interest and was more than intrigued. She hadn't felt this sort of excitement since leaving Korea.

"We just need to take the lift to level four of this building," he said and he started to move.

They got in, the lift empty apart from a couple of corporate workers and two women dressed in blue, the shirts and skirts obviously a uniform but smart indeed. He inserted a key and hit 'rooftop', which lit up with a sign saying 'access allowed'. They travelled in seconds to the top floor. As the lift came to a slow stop, the doors opened and they walked out into an empty room. There was light bouncing off every surface; the walls, the ceilings, the beams. There were angles on angles and warmth on cool. It was absolutely stunning and for the second time today she was reminded of Korea and the vibrancy that it offered. Transfixed, she was lost in the moment, taken back in time to when she first found out that Shane had been cheating, that her life in Korea was over. What was with today and all the memories of Korea engulfing her suffocation her.

She remembered how her heart was pounding as she walked into the "TBar" on the nightlife strip, both her and Shane's favourite hangout. She knew there was something to be concerned about but forcefully tried to shake it off. She was sure he shouldn't be there.

What lay ahead wasn't something she wanted to know, but knew she had to know. She walked down the long marbled corridor of TBar, winding around pillars and the overwhelming magnificent entrance. Bracing herself, she remembered vividly considering not going in at all. She loved that bar and they had had so many memories there; she didn't want that ruined. The room was outstanding, the fit-out timeless. She had travelled far and wide but that place was by far her favourite - it was his too. TBar was an acquired taste and everyone had an opinion, you either loved it or hated it and it became the Kevin Bacon of expats in Korea. Those who loved it, owned it and defended it ruthlessly while the others had a thousand more places to choose from. If what she had been told was true why didn't Shane choose another place, then at least it could have remained hers, she would still have been able to go there freely, safely. She took a deep breath; her beloved steel door slid open and she entered. The maître de handed her a glass of champagne, she smiled. She walked past the huge glass structured ivy as water fell noiselessly down from the ceiling through the ivy and into the pink pearl pond at the base. She tipped her champagne out into it. Her heart had stopped, she thought "This is what it must be like to have a heart attack, this is what I'm having. My life is being destroyed right in front of me and this is how finally it is going to end." A heart attack in Tbar, miles from home. She realised she was not overly distressed by the idea, in fact she found the solution a relief. Holding on to a huge mosaic pink tiled vase she steadied herself and finally looked around. She couldn't see him and, relieved, she thought quickly to turn around and leave. She looked further, still nothing. Maybe her information was wrong. Maybe it was a dream and she would wake and things would be as they were. That's what she would do, go home and wake up and everything would be alright again. And then she saw him. The dream was shattered and everything her friend had told her was there, right in front of her. Him and her, his boss and her fiancé, kissing close and intimately.

"Are you alright, Audrey?" A gentle touch on the arm from Ian brought her back around.

"Wow," she finally managed to say, embarrassed that she had gone there, wondering how long he might have been looking at her.

"What a room. Sorry, I was just taking it all in, it reminds of another time in a great bar in Seoul."

Ian nodded and walked ahead of her around to the left. She now saw a circular structure and realised it was probably the carcass of the bar. There were papers, drawings, designs everywhere and she could see straight away what was going on.

"A restaurant?" Audrey asked.

"Yes," he said, "what do you think?"

He was looking at her with such intensity that she assumed it was his. She had misread him and wondered if he knew anything about running restaurants. The look on her face may have prompted him to confide.

"The owners don't know I'm talking to you. I want to be honest about that but I think they could use a hand with the some of the design details and I hear you're pretty good at this sort of thing." He shuffled his feet, his eyes not leaving her face.

She absorbed this new information, everything making far more sense, and looked from him to the beautiful space and the stunning vista outside. The city at this time was dynamite and in an hour or two when the sun started to set the view from up here would be priceless. "What a cracking spot for a restaurant," she thought. Who knew? She could see it all, easily. She spent a fair bit of time in restaurants and bars around the globe; there was one good part to being single. She hated cooking, and after Shane she had no one to cook for anyway and enjoyed a night out. Korea had added to her sense of design in a city where more and more and more created nothing less than magic. This would be amazing no doubt, there were so many ideas running through her mind, so many possibilities. "Hold on," she reminded herself, he wasn't even the owner - maybe the builder or an investor, a friend. He had to sell her to them, the owners. She didn't know if she needed this. Such a serious commitment to something easily non-committal at this stage. Could she be bothered? She would have to produce concepts, which took time, research, money. However, given the appeal of the room and the natural elements that came with it, she knew there probably wasn't much architecturally that she needed to do. But if it was the architect he wanted, it would just be a matter of adding to what was already present. She could feel this place in her bones, she wanted to sit down on the bare floorboards and draw under the ray of light coming in through the window. This place made her feel young again, optimistic, beautiful even. She felt like someone could fall in love with her here, could see the beauty in her that hadn't been seen in so long. She was committed - without their approval she was already involved. This room needed her, she needed it. She wanted him to go, to leave her alone, let nightfall happen so she could see the twinkling of lights across the river, across to the areas on the hill. She could see herself sitting in there, more right to be there than maybe even these owners, privileged, more worthy as the design would be hers. She would bring her sister, her mother and of course her father, she'd be recognised, acknowledged. This would be her way back from Korea. They would be proud of her, maybe for the first time ever they would be genuinely proud that she contributed to something that they could show their friends. Sure it wasn't a husband or children, but it was tangible and it was a trophy of some sort. Their friends would be impressed. Her family loved dining out, only at the great restaurants though, quick to visit when a new one opened. They never went on their own her mother and father, they would invite friends and family and spend an exorbitant amount of money. They would critique, review and sound like authorities on food and wine. Money was never an issue, the bill huge, the tip, should there be enough people watching, was generous. This would be right up their alley.

Ian appeared at her side and she jumped, startled, not expecting him as she was so absorbed in her fairy tale, possibly her future. He showed her the existing plans, explained the general layout. As he spoke she watched him move; his mannerisms, warm emotions that she didn't expect. He moved around the room comfortably, loyally as he explained a table here, the site of the toilets there, the line of the kitchen. His passion and belief in the project was infectious and she lost herself in his performance. He told her about the owners; two girls who were highly intelligent, astute and really inspiring. He continued on without a glance about their fierce involvement in all aspects of this restaurant, they were adamant to go it alone, had done all of the design work themselves.

He looked at her finally, "Don't get me wrong, they have a great eye for it - but perhaps there's an opportunity for something more, some definite expertise."

He was convinced the venue had the ability to be the best in the city - maybe the country - and he didn't want them to overlook a single finish. Looking at her shyly he realised he had exposed himself.

"This will truly be a fantastic restaurant, the girls have an energy and partnership together that I've never seen before. I know I'm only the builder but they trust me and I trust them and if I don't at least try to help them I will regret it for the rest of my life." He looked down at his hands and started fidgeting.

Audrey was in. He had taken her away to a place that she distantly remembered. A time when the moment you were in was all that mattered. When you knew you were a part of something bigger, someone bigger. People relied on you, valued you and what you had to offer. A time when having children and a blissful marriage were all ahead of her. It had been a long time since she felt like a part of something, solidly. Who were these girls? He spoke of them wistfully, magically, ethereally. They weren't his family, he was just their builder, and yet they had this effect on him. Maybe they were closer than she knew, a girlfriend perhaps? But he seemed to be in awe of them both, like a recent acquaintance. "Whatever the situation," she thought, she was in. How did they find this sexy space? He said they had experience and intelligence but did they really know how to run a restaurant of this scale? Her old self popped up: "They probably don't," she smirked to herself, Daddy's money - which she knew well enough - or a rich boyfriend or husband. They couldn't be as amazing as this Ian character was carrying on about.

"I'll have to think about it. It is strange to quote a job that's not actually a job yet. There's a lot of work involved in producing a quote to be told by a 'potential' client that they were never interested in the first place."

"The girls are smart," he said quickly. "If you give them something good, they won't back away from it. If nothing comes of it, you can charge me for your time."

She pretended not to hear the last bit - like she wouldn't provide something good? She had lived in one of the most vibrant restaurant districts in the world, Korea. This town had nothing on what the Koreans could put together for a single buck.

"Right, well there it is then. I'll get to work and we'll meet with the owners. I'll be ready in four or five days. You can email me the blueprints tonight?" she asked efficiently.

"Of course. I'll do it now."

They shook hands and she left, making way for a table where a computer sat. Stepping out of the lift it hit her again how many people there were coming and going from this little corner of the city. A goldmine – he was right, these girls could be smart.

Chapter Five

There hadn't been a huge amount of questions asked by her family, friends or colleagues. The story seemed to sell; her father was meticulous with that sort of thing, it was Christian's strength. It was fair though, Audrey thought, that she should have been compensated; he had hurt her and she had given him everything. Well, almost everything. She had supported Shane all through his finals. He studied the whole last year, never going out, never going on any trips, holidays, he turned into a hermit overnight and then left her as one too. Most of their social life was through him, she knew that - without him she seemed not to exist. It crippled her, the rejection. Sure she had a few friends of her own but he was the connected one, the networked one. Not only had he switched their relationship off like pulling the plug out of a charger but his company, that he spent all their time on building, found its legs and was absolutely killing it. His world had started moving in leaps and bounds and after he completed his studies everyone was saying it was simply going to increase tenfold. She had been happy to stick around, put up with it, even though they literally had had no life in the last two years. He kept assuring her that it was going to be worth millions and all the long hours would pay off. In truth, she was pumped. She had fled to Korea in part because she was bored but mainly to put as many miles between her and the prying, disappointed eyes of her family. Childless & husbandless she had gone in search of validity, verification that she could do it, that she could produce what her family was expecting of her. She hadn't believed her luck when he asked her out at work only a month or so after she arrived. They had a fun night. There weren't fireworks but she was long over expecting that and somehow the relationship continued. They enjoyed each other's company, liked similar things, and slowly she became part of his life. It was definitely his life, but that suited her, she was new to the city so someone established was perfect. His friends became her friends, his interests hers and even though she felt fairly anonymous at times and if she was honest, unnecessary a lot of the other time, he kept her on. When it was just the two of them it worked fine. Everyone had met him and approved instantly. Of course he hadn't travelled home, the family had journeyed there to meet him but it had been a great success and then he asked her to marry him. Of course she said yes, she would make the best of it and no one else was asking. She knew she should have been more jubilant, ecstatic and appreciative but what she mainly felt was relief. Their love life was dim and it always had been, but this in itself was not the main problem - she was more concerned with the lack of concern they felt about it. They didn't fight over it, analyse it, or even discuss it. There weren't two definite sides like she had read about most couples, him always wanting and her always too tired. He never really asked for it and she never really offered. She wasn't surprised by her attitude - sex and sexual behaviour was something she had never really been into. If she never had sex again it wouldn't upset her. Her past boyfriends had, on reflection, been far more obliging than Shane but even then she could take it or leave it. When she had flatted with girls she would hear them, groaning, yelping with whomever ended up in their beds. She often wondered what all the fuss was about. They loved to sit at the end of her bed the next night and tell her all the intimate details. She would listen intently and they questioned her, asked if she even felt the slightest bit aroused by their stories of sex and sweat. Of course she said yes, but only because they were telling the story. On one occasion the screamer in the house had pulled her into her bedroom, her boyfriend lying naked on the bed with a massive hard-on. She let her take off her shirt and kiss her but when she suggested jumping onto the bed too she had declined, saying thanks all the same, and went back to her room wondering who had initiated what. Still, she had felt something very much that night and had finished the job; thinking of her flatmate, not her boyfriend.

No, her relationship with Shane had never been one of lust, never filled with hours and hours of endless sex and romping. They were efficient and to the point and no one complained. If he was unhappy she figured he would have told her.

Two months before the wedding he took her out to dinner and explained how manic business was. The company had taken off as predicted, almost tripling in size but so quickly, so unexpectedly. His new work schedule was excruciating and he had little time for anything else. She held his hand and said she understood, they would get through it just like before. She nurtured him with warmth and care saying she knew what was ahead and he didn't have to worry about her. Soon they would be pregnant and she'd raise the family and he could be the businessman – that's just how it is in Korea. He had cried saying he wished that was it, he wished that's how it could be but it couldn't. He had been wrong, he was so so sorry. All he had wanted was his business to be a success and now it was. A huge success but it was at the expense of his marriage - well, his pending marriage.

"What do you mean?" she had said softly.

He couldn't do it to her, he couldn't ask her to live that life, take away from her all that she deserved of a husband at her side. He couldn't expect her to marry him, he had to focus on the business and he couldn't consciously do both, so the marriage was off.

Gutted and humiliated, in disbelief she sat there, stunned. Too stunned to speak. He continued on but she didn't hear him, couldn't even see him. She had been there every step of the way just to be tossed aside at the eleventh hour. The invitations had been sent, huge amounts of money had been paid. People were coming from far away. This was her moment.

He would attend to everyone, he told her. He would take full blame and he was so sad for himself that he could only see his future as being married to his work. He couldn't go back though, he couldn't depart from it and he knew within himself that he couldn't do both, there was just not enough of him. Their prawns arrived and they both stared at their plates.

She solemnly swore to herself that it wouldn't be the end and it hadn't been. By the time she packed her life up and sent it home, she had robbed him of millions and he was none the wiser. One small change on the digits for the weekly payments to their saving account, had been it all took. The grant was being paid daily in random amounts from his major four big clients and she had simply adjusted the transactions to pay half of every payment into a second account. She had accidently done it once before, a true accident when he asked her to submit the paperwork. Four hundred and two thousand American dollars had gone into her car loan account. It took her six months to realise her account was in credit and unless she had told him she was pretty sure he wouldn't have realised at all. So she set up a pseudo company, transferred the bank account details and left with 1.2 million dollars tucked away. She had intended to cancel the account when she was leaving, knowing that tracing international funds was much easier, but she couldn't, so she took the money and changed the formula to only one payment a week, into another account which was held in Korea just in case.

She feared her arrival home, the toughest part yet to come, and as usual she wasn't disappointed. Her mother's look said it all, Gareth said nothing and feeling like a ten year old she rode home in the back of her parents' car.

Chapter Six

Annika grabbed her towel from the side of the pool, exhausted, and walked back to the change rooms. She took a seat on the bench next to the lockers, and leaning back into the wall closed her eyes. Her towel was wrapped firmly around her. The police force taught her many things but swimming was the one that she really found a love for; as soon as she hit the water, she entered a safe place, the world outside her washed away, distant in space somewhere. She learnt a lot about people at the Academy, many running from something, impressing someone. Everyone had a past, she knew that, and everyone had skeletons in their closet, no matter how squeaky-clean you were. So she had a story too but so did the next person and she was on a comeback, was close to getting back to herself, whoever that was. Ultimately she decided that she had come out, at the age of thirty-five, ahead of the game. There was too much assault, abuse and aggression in her line of work and she was glad to be moving on. She spent enough time in that world not only as the hero but as the victim too. She knew she would always look over her shoulder but she came to terms with that, she manoeuvred herself into a routine that allowed the anxiety. It didn't concern her anymore, she was now trained to prevent it, even enforce it. She was finally starting to feel safe. Years later, after fleeing the orphanage, fleeing her sick tormentor, fleeing herself, she had won. She had survived the police force in fact finished top of her class and finally had emerged mentally and physically as a new person. She had reinvented herself, thank god, knowing that if she hadn't, her fate would be sealed.

I was the only person who knew what her previous life had been. Annika told me the whole story, not leaving a detail out. I never pushed or probed her and she was thankful to me for that. The most amazing woman she had had the privilege of knowing had been her guardian angel and she couldn't have believed her luck to have met me as well. Sitting in the café, backpack next to me, gazing out over the ocean looking apparently serene and wise. She said she owed me for where she was now. She thought I could have taught some of the men at the academy a thing or two, I was a powerhouse of compassion and resilience. By the end of the first week we met we had both talked and talked, confessed and cried, bonding instantly. It was impossible not to be drawn to her, she was raw and honest and expected nothing in return. All she asked was that you were honest too. She mirrored so much of what I myself had felt, all those emotions and heartache from constantly fleeing places and feeling so afraid she had put into words so poetically. Now, five years later, we were in business together, I mean, hell, serious business, opening a restaurant. She didn't have the first clue about running a restaurant let alone owning one, but I convinced her, trusted her, believed in her and she was having the time of her life. Finally, she was living in the moment for herself and she was exhilarated by the pure simplicity of it. Not that the job was simple but the living was. The waking up every day and going to bed every night had become simple, normal and she savoured it daily. Somehow she ended up taking on the role of a sort of project manager. It was true, I said there should only be one contact, ideally one person in charge or before you know it you'll have doubled the workload and halved the results. It seemed her organisational skills were better with people and places, not details and dates, so she had just fallen into it and risen to the occasion too, wanting to make me proud and finding out along the way she was actually quite good at it.

Her relationship with the builder started out rocky but with time and patience they managed to connect and on some occasions she had even contributed some genuinely good ideas. She could see the restaurant every time she stepped into the room, constantly amazed that she was a part of it, a huge part, that her life had taken this bizarre path. She knew that if she got hit by a car tomorrow she would go happy, happy at how it had all finally ended. She couldn't have asked for any of it, yet here it was, hers fairly and squarely.

She shivered; the temperature had dropped. Looking around she stripped out of her swimmers and took a hot shower. Dressed, she made her way to the café where her always-on-time best friend and business partner was waiting.

"These pictures are amazing Ann, you must have been at it all night, you had none of this when I left you yesterday."

"Well I'm no designer but it does seem to be taking some shape," she said, agreeing casually. "Hopefully they'll work in the room."

"Cooking is design, Ann, you have a natural talent for it. Sure you may not be industry-trained but being creative is being creative, you wouldn't be half the chef you are if you weren't creative."

"Thanks Sass, really, you should be in PR - you always know the right thing to say." She hugged me.

I laughed, "Tom used to say that, but more in a negative way I think."

Annika looked at me closely. "I doubt that Sass, you're the least negative person I know and from what I've heard, Tom thought so too."

I shrugged and finished my coffee, Annika noticing the vacant look she got whenever his name was mentioned.

Changing the subject she announced: "Let's head up?"

I never tired of the room; stepping out of the lift neither of us spoke, both savouring the feel. The weather was still good but the light

163

outside would soon fade and with it bring about yet another feel. It was what attracted me to it originally. Depending on what was happening outside, it completely reflected the atmosphere inside. Annie and I thought long and hard about how to use this in the fit-out. The huge windows were the soul of the room, with magnificent arches and intricate timber work. Some still had their original stained-glass, pearl-like patterns filtering through the glass and others had smaller sections of the window that could be opened like little cat doors. The whole effect was like a Christmas tree with ornate decorations dangling from its limbs. My favourite time was always late in the night, when it was quiet and dark. We had convinced the landlords to add the latest and greatest awnings from a German designer to the façade. They just covered the tips of the windows, shading the sun but not the light. The result was perfect, the landlords liking them so much that they installed them throughout the building.

One could only access the floor of the restaurant via the lift with a code, in the foyer the receptionist manned the phones and the activities of the other floor. She had been vetting endless enquiries regarding the restaurant and had been kind enough to start a log, emailing me on a daily basis the details. It was a huge bonus for a restaurant, where business was mainly website-driven, not so much through actual contact. Therese was her name; she soon became a close friend.

Something caught my eye in the reflection and I moved through the room around to the bar area. Ian was leaning over the bar, head down, engrossed in papers and boards on the table. By his side was a lady talking to him in quiet tones, head bent similarly over the same table. They looked serious so I walked back to Ann, leaving them to it until she left. There were always extras onsite coming and going with various requirements and you could never judge a person by their appearance; sometimes the most glamorous women were selling meat and the most nondescript, passable women were importing the finest crystals. Normally Ian would act slightly dismissive, vaguely interested. Listen politely for their five-minute grab then decline apologetically, accepting their brochures anyway, offering them a glimmer of hope. However he looked genuinely interested, involved, concentrating on what she was saying in hushed tones. I left them to it, not wanting to interrupt and headed back to Ann. As I turned around we bumped into each other and she looked over my shoulder.

"Who's with Ian?" she asked.

"No idea, sales pitch?" I said. "I'm just going to check on the disabled loo, apparently the inspector came whilst I was out and left the report on the door." I wandered off and Ann walked in the opposite direction.

"I'm just going to check on the lady with the exquisite shoes, next to Ian!" she said, and I left her to it.

She was wearing the most beautiful shoes Annika had ever seen and as she looked closer she noticed her handbag and briefcase were equally as gorgeous. She looked younger than Annika but it was hard to tell exactly how young from the angle she was standing. Her curiosity got the better of her and she walked closer.

"Hey Ian, hope I'm not interrupting, just thought I'd let you know we were here."

Before he could speak the lady looked up and turned to face her, only inches from each other. The lady stared straight through her and she felt an odd sensation. She felt like she had just walked in on a very private moment and instantly regretted it, wishing she was anywhere else. Exposing what they had both been poring over, Ian made a move away from the lady and she looked beyond them both to the table. She quickly looked twice, not at the young lady but at the images on the table and recognised immediately the room, the drawings. The lady looked up at her curiously, almost with surprise, like a ghost had entered the room. She held the lady's eyes, startled at the soul she was staring into.

Chapter Seven

As the lady looked up Annika felt a shiver, like someone had walked over her grave. She turned back to the drawings laid on the table, unable to look away. Ian started to speak but she wasn't paying much attention. There was something about an architect, some suggestions, just to look at. She couldn't shake a strange feeling, not sure if it had something to do with what she was looking at or the change in the air. It felt like there was an intruder in the room but she couldn't assign it to the artwork or the moment. She was mesmerised by the drawings. Saw it as clear as day. This woman had captured exactly what we had felt the day we stood side by side looking into the room, the future. It was breathtaking and Annika for a moment wondered, "How much time has this lady spent here?" How could she possibly have captured all of this in one visit? Her concern was overshadowed by her enthusiasm and greed for what she saw on the paper. She instantly wanted it, knew it would transform their original plans into the Rolls Royce of restaurants. It would catapult them on to a new level, a level of stardom, a serious platform, worthy of the world stage. Who was this woman with her extraordinary ideas, her obvious extreme talent, her complete genius?

Ian tapped her on the shoulder. "Annika, can I introduce you to Audrey? These are her drawings." Annika, with great hesitation and a murmur that seemed to be in slow motion, shifted her gaze from the plans to the lady.

"Hi Annika, absolute pleasure to meet you," the bubbliest voice sang at her. "You have the most stunning space for a restaurant. I hope you like what I've come up with?"

167

Annika looked at Ian for explanation, guidance. She didn't want to speak, afraid of what she might say. She needed me, this was my domain. Always capable of gaining and keeping control. Never appearing on the back foot; confident, in charge. She was not prepared for this and felt completely out of her depth. She loved the designs but had no idea how to handle it with both of them looking at her, it was their dream after all.

"Hi Audrey," she managed. "Lovely to meet you."

She extended her hand, not knowing what else to do. Ian, realising that Annika was unsure of this impromptu meeting, called me over.

"Sass, do you have a moment? I'd like to introduce you to Audrey, I've asked her to do some sketches for me, just to make sure we haven't missed anything. You know, get a second opinion on some of the structures, finishes. She's been drawing restaurants in various locations for over five years."

"Hi, Audrey," I took over.

"I know this is a bit unexpected but Ian rang me to ask if I would have a look over your plans for your new restaurant. I simply fell in love with the space and couldn't stop thinking about it. I know you have plans already so no harm if they're not what you're looking for, but it was pleasure enough just putting the concepts together. This is a dream for an architect, the building is outstanding," she finished, smiling broadly at us both.

Immediately taking charge, I moved closer. "Thank you, Audrey was it? We think it's a beautiful spot too, we're glad you agree. You've met my business partner Annika Osborne. We own the project together." I always included her, making sure everyone knew we were in it together, equal even though she thought I was the drawcard, the name, the reputation, I never omitted her on any occasion, it wasn't about me.

"Umm, absolutely, yes, just now."

In true me-style, I shifted the authority back to me and the woman felt it, stumbling a little with her response. "Well then, Ann, should we take a look?" I turned the pages of the oversized sketchpad next to the storyboard. "If this lady has taken the trouble to ponder our little restaurant we could certainly, at least, return the favour?"

Annika smiled, nodding, knowing as soon as I took a look I would see exactly what she herself had seen a little earlier. She kept her head down towards the sketches, close to me, lightly touching my elbow. I took my time looking at the drawings, flipping pages, consulting the storyboard. No one spoke. Annika knew the drawings were amazing, way beyond what the two of us had expected - it was how I was going to handle it that Annika was unsure of.

"I like what you've done with the corner window," I said to Audrey, moving items off the plans to turn them around so they faced the same direction as the room.

"It seemed like an instant feature," Audrey said. "It stood out the day I met Ian, as a focal point, a point where everyone's eyes in the room could gravitate to, particularly if there was a break in the table conversation or the need for a distraction topic. You know how it gets sometimes at dinner; awkward moments."

"I totally agree, it gives the corner definition. What do you think Ann?" I looked at her to play along. She could see the fire in my eyes always blazing like that when I was excited about something.

"Absolutely," said Annika, "it was the one area the jury was still out on hey Sass, we were wondering what to put in that corner."

"Mmm, we couldn't quite piece it together, could we?" I was muttering more to myself and Ann.

Audrey spoke up, "I think the bar area could also be improved with some curtaining, beading - something to separate the areas, create more niches, little corners for who knows what."

"Mmm" I said, "the last restaurant we did, had a bar similar to that but we were trying to stay away from it this time round. Do you think it is back in fashion, still edgy enough?" I asked, making it sound genuine enough.

"It's an option, that's all," said Audrey, "most things are cyclical in design so often last year's news can be this year's news, but in a different colour."

"Well the designs are certainly terrific, clearly Ian was steered in the right direction by whoever recommended you, but unfortunately Annika and I have one of those ghastly meetings with liquor licensing and it does you no favours to keep them waiting. If you agree we would love to keep the designs, have a look over them and give you a call sometime tomorrow to touch base?"

"No problem," she said, "my details are on the drawings and here's my card, so call me when you have a moment. I'd be thrilled to discuss the concepts with you in more detail."

Annika and I took her card and she left, stepping into the lift, smiling as the doors closed.

"Well," Audrey thought, "I have no idea what to make of that at all." They were clearly best friends as well as business partners, their absolute respect and enjoyment for one another so obvious. As the lift descended she realised she couldn't say either way whether she would ever hear from them again.

I turned to Ian. "We'll be back in an hour or two depending on how long it takes, will you still be here?"

"Ah no, I've got to pick up the paint, they sent the wrong colour." He was about to continue but I waved him off.

"See you in the morning then." I took the lift downstairs.

Down on the footpath, Annika turned to me. "Sorry Sass, completely forgot about the meeting."

I laughed, "No honey, sorry it's my fault, there is no meeting. I just needed to get you and I out of there so we could breathe! Where did that lady come from? I know you saw it too, those drawings were amazing, they jumped off the paper."

We walked across the road and into the gardens that lined the city, hiding the huge lake that lay beyond, the city forming the river bend. We discussed Audrey's drawings, excitedly but with trepidation. It was our project, our chance to shed our outer layers, fly free with a new beginning. We had not bargained on a third party and now with the introduction of a designer it would automatically become hers as well. She would have to be included in discussions, considerations, successes, failures. It turned our holistic approach into a standard business model and we weren't sure if it was worth it. Of course even as we walked in silence we knew it would be foolish not to engage her, knowing that now we'd seen what it could be, it simply had to be. It would be the difference between great and outstanding. It was sadly, after all, a business, and we had come too far to not commit to the best it could possibly be.

"Well, that's that then hey Sass," Annika said flatly.

"Yep my love, that's that Ann," I responded.

We headed back to our room and instinctively I opened a bottle of chilled Chablis that had arrived earlier as a gift to the two of us for a fantastic piece in the paper earlier that day. With a heavy heart and a haunting feeling we looked over her designs, her remarkable designs and quietly held our glasses. There should have been great excitement between us, tremendous hope for this new look, for the amazing transformation she had made to our intimate project. But all that hung in the air tonight, all that hovered above the bar, above the street below, the great lake sprawled out under the trees, shimmering wildly in the night air through the windows, was a feeling of sadness, a great cloud of grief for what could have been and a static that neither of us could understand.

Chapter Eight

Ian, Annika and Audrey were deep in conversation and there was no time for details, so I headed out, not wanting to interrupt them. They wouldn't miss me, the restaurant was getting close to completion, and I was hesitant to interrupt anyway, knowing the stress everyone was under. The taste of the pungent Roquefort still lingered in my mouth and meshed my lips together, and I attempted to savour the taste for as long as it lasted. I had ordered inordinate amounts of it for the opening night after finding some of the best in Paris at a tasting Thierry had organised. The trouble – well, loosely called that if you considered it trouble - was finding the perfect French Sparkling to match it for the toast. I decided on the Sathenay Cremant de Bourgogne Brut after sampling some more than impressive drops and negotiating a great price for the restaurant in Paris too. As I hurried down the street I knew a carton would turn up tomorrow as a gift, a gesture to say thank you and thought rather ruthlessly, "Good, I'll add that to the opening night stock." There was a huge amount of complimentary stock already on offer, getting me through the first month but every bottle counted. Anyone who came sniffing around was instantly charmed at the restaurant and word had got out. It had finally started to take some form now and everyone seemed overly impressed. It was hard to imagine the fit-out now without Audrey's touch - the space had taken on a different quality, one with sophistication that might not have otherwise been there. Suppliers and distributers were knocking on the door, offering aggressive deals and donations, knowing the opening was only months away.

The wind struck up a bit as I headed left onto Warrik Street, I was thinking of Annika. Her and Ian had become like brother and sister, affectionately mucking around and equally arguing points like their life depended on it. His girlfriend Poppy had also become tight with her and together they shared a great bond. Poppy, I laughed, she had tried to set Annie up with a handful of Ian's mates but nothing stuck. Ann confessed to Poppy she wasn't all that interested in a boyfriend. She loved meeting new people and being a part of the wider world but a partner wasn't a priority for her at the moment and eventually poor Poppy gave up, realising she was fighting a losing battle. Poppy and Ian had fallen pregnant with their first child so luckily for Annika's sake her love life had easily taken a back seat. They had asked Annika to be the godmother, crying when the moment arrived. I knew Annie didn't want to live the rest of her life alone but she held a strong force-field around her and I somehow thought, that guard would only be broken by the right one. How she found the right one without breaking the guard was merely a small part of the equation. I understood, it would happen when she was ready. She had enjoyed more than anything the contact with Ian. Having a male friendship in her life, completely platonic, without a hint of anything further was deeply soul-restoring for her. I envied it. She had no brother, no sister and he had filled a void, as much as an outsider could. Funnily, Tom and I had always believed, had agreed on often, that men and women existed solely in a sexual framework. Friendship between two single people was complete crap, impossible for two unattached sexes both of the same desire to cohabit platonically. It was rife with sexual undertones, this stemmed from the stone age and it was impossible for the modern world to change, as much as it might try.

I knew wholeheartedly that Annika was not attracted to Ian but as much as he loved Poppy, I couldn't say for absolute certainty the same was true of him. Not that he ever showed anything but warmth, but if I wasn't mistaken somewhere along the way a strange sort of sexual tension had arisen within the group. I hadn't been able to put my finger on it. I knew Poppy had become pregnant and that Ian was chuffed, wrapped up in it completely. Whilst they weren't actually married I knew that that was a moral issue, not a commitment issue, but he was the only male in the team. Not once had I felt this current in the group before, yet I was sure something existed now. Of course Audrey was added to the team now, and Poppy's pregnancy, but I couldn't see how that would change anything. Still, the single factor was that the only male was Ian, so then did it mean it had to be between him and someone? Maybe it was all in my head, maybe it was as simple as Ian feeling differently now that he was a step away from fatherhood. It didn't seem right but what else could it be?

I pressed the doorbell on Martha Street number 106 and the sommelier opened the door. He took my coat and handed me a glass of Larmandier Champagne. "Ahh," I thought, "back to more important matters, our house pate." I shrugged off my feelings; if there was anything going on time would tell, and in my experience it always did.

Chapter Nine

Audrey's union had formed rather effortlessly. She had found her niche in the group and slotted in. She was casual enough without being complacent and stern enough without being overbearing. She laughed when appropriate and knuckled-down when needed. There wasn't a great deal more to her than that. She was quite predictable, not offensive nor overwhelming. On paper she ticked all the boxes and was obviously very talented. Her intelligence was more learned than natural yet she got by fine. Her style was that of an artistic professional, and one day she would arrive in genuine vintage Chanel, the next an Asian rip-off. She would dress bohemian, vagabond and still shoulder her Louis Vuitton satchel. Her leather goods on the other hand were impeccable, causing us to drool over them daily. We would smell and stroke them until it became a bit embarrassing. She had an equally amazing jewellery collection. Always there was jewellery hanging off her ears, neck, wrists. Fake, imported, bling or timber, ceramic or compositions. She drove the latest Audi convertible which on her art-house days reeked of a parents' car (which it was) and on her glamour days seemed to complete her. She had mousey brown hair, set in a longish bob often worn pulled back with various bobby pins and her eyes were set back into her face, widely apart, the colour of mocha. Her face was almost round and slightly pale. She wasn't unattractive but no stand out, she walked every second morning and when she drank, she smoked. She came from a highly successful family of overachievers and her parents were still together and madly in love. Apparently she had been engaged before but she had called it off at the eleventh hour, citing she couldn't match the love of her parents, making her slightly admirable. Whatever had happened, there were certainly very few men around now. She said men were threatened by her but maybe they were just bored by her. The opposite of Annie, she waited on every corner block looking, hoping for the next one but no one was to be found. She had one girlfriend who hooked her up regularly enough but after one or two dates the end would happen.

The opening party was looming and I was sure her date would be another lost cause, going nowhere. Some of the men she had introduced us to had been great. Sure they always looked twice at Annie, but that was usual. When we would enquire as to how they were going, she would shake her head 'not the one' sometimes only after their first date. She had started dating a guy called Mark who, just like her, looked great on paper. He had been rather charming and appeared attentive to her, listening when she spoke, laughing when she laughed. We had been over the moon for her. Every month there was discussion about if this was the 'one', was she getting any good vibes for you-know-what. The whole office was supportive, quietly encouraging her to pursue the relationship, steadily not forcefully. Poppy always mentioned his name whenever she came in to see Ian or to fuss over her pregnant belly. The relationship had lasted longer than any others and there was great hope that this was it, finally. They would marry, have children and she could stop the manhunt that consumed her. She confessed to Annika that maybe she had been too hasty in breaking up with her partner in Korea, how hard it had been to find someone like him again. Alas, Mark was not to be either and within a day we were not allowed to speak his name. She was really starting to worry now, she couldn't possibly attend the opening without a partner, even though Annika and Sass were. She wished she could pretend to be with them, a threesome, the three girls fighting on their own but it wasn't like that. It was the two girls fighting on their own and she was the employee. All the press raved about Annie and Sass like a global brand and Audrey knew she wasn't a part of that. She was much closer with Annie in fact adored Annie but she had not really connected with Sass. She had no problem with Sass, admired her actually, but she had kept her distance, she had made it blatantly clear it was business they were in together not friendship. She often caught Sass looking at her in a strange way, a way that made her shiver like she could read her mind. Audrey was in fact sure there wasn't too much the wonder woman couldn't do. But Annika on the other hand was a pure delight. They would go for coffee together, shop together and she felt she could tell her anything. She thought even one day she might confide in her the truth about what happened in Korea, the theft, the exfiance not the story her dad had invented. She was convinced Annika of all people would understand, and she realised she was quite desperate to have Annika as her confidant, have her impressed with what Audrey could actually do if she was pushed. She longed for the day when she could tell her about her parents, her family, the sad pathetic truth of it all. It would be a great relief and Annika was so trustworthy she knew she was the right person, but in the meanwhile she needed to find someone to come to the party with her.

Chapter Ten

We met Audrey's parents the day after we signed her contract. They arrived with her, holding Tiffany's bags, a gift for both me and Annika to celebrate our new venture. We had been floored but they wouldn't take no for an answer, making her father quite upset. Eventually we relented but found it to be very uncomfortable. Their faces had seemed vaguely familiar at the time. I wasn't sure of course, having had many patrons over the years, but oddly something about them made me think I had seen them before a long time ago, well before I had been in restaurants. I knew Audrey was a good few years older than us and I struggled to think where we could have crossed paths. I was pretty sure I hadn't met Audrey before so maybe it had something to do with her older sister or her parents themselves. Either way, they were exactly as I expected her parents to be. Wealthy, affluent, established, distinguished. She was elegant and then some, he was regal in stature and in his presence. It was so far from what I grew up with, how my childhood presented. I had long since realised everyone has a story and anyone who doesn't, usually wants one. I accepted mine a long time ago, with the passing of my father first and then not so long ago, Tom. I had actually learnt to welcome my past, my lineage, knowing it had given me the courage and resilience to get me through what I had been through.

They were the nuclear family, that was obvious; the providing stable husband, the mother to the children, the wife of their domain. Their appearance was at contrast to their demeanour. He acted almost humbly, like a passenger on a train, a tourist with a tour guide, the destination determined by anyone other than himself. He constantly referred to 'the girls' like he was their puppet, like they were in charge, he was on their leash. Yet clearly no one, least of all his wife, believed it. They sought reassurance with any word they uttered. They urged his opinion on any matter, they agreed whenever he spoke. It was quite enthralling to watch, even entertaining. I wondered who they were trying to fool - us or themselves? I imagined it had been going on since the beginning of time, yet strangely amidst their constant dialogue the mother's voice was vacant. She spoke of Audrey's elder sister with nervousness. We knew of her success and achievements, she had three kids and a doctor for a husband but still there was a certain gravity in the woman's voice, like a heavy burden this very successful child was to her. She was clearly a devoted grandmother but it felt like facts that were rolling off her tongue.

Her father Christian began to appear regularly. He dropped in often to say hi, look at the progress or catch up with Audrey, whether or not she was on hand. His visits at the beginning were neither welcomed nor unwelcomed and as time went on they became part of the routine. He was around more than he was not. One week Audrey was not needed yet he had visited every day. He would inspect, observe, query. He and Ian had found some common ground, the builder and the barrister, quickly transforming his visits from a quick hello to an overseer. It had happened so quietly, so subtly that no one thought it unusual. He was firmly expected and firmly consulted. Audrey had embraced his involvement, speaking of him constantly, ringing him with questions and advice. He contributed & supported but somewhere along the way, somewhere along the line their partnership had muddied. Now they were four, all in it together. We had attended their birthdays, been invited for dinner, even shared a small holiday together. Now looking down at the spreadsheet, his voice is forever present in her head,

"I get the feeling Christian would have a different opinion on this," she said as she examined the spreadsheet.

"Is it just me Annie, or are we spending a lot of time these days discussing what Christian would or wouldn't say?"

"Well it is a bit like that, but he makes such sense. There are definitely areas where he knows infinitely better than us and he's saving us a bomb using his company and connections."

"Yeah but at what price," I muttered.

"Pardon love?"

"I said I know but at what price?"

"How do you mean Sass?"

"Oh nothing – it's my bitterness, my cynicism. I just get the feeling we're in this way over our heads and I don't even know what 'in this' is but I find myself asking, 'when did he become so involved?' I mean he's now more involved than Audrey," I said, shaking my head.

"Do you think it's a problem Sass?" she genuinely asked. "I mean, you think there's something going on? What could possibly be going on? When the fit-out's done, so is she and so is he. It's pretty straightforward. I think he's just chuffed to be involved in something with his daughter and vice versa."

"That's right, so why can't they find something of their own to get involved in, why in our life? I'm not saying I'm ungrateful, he has been amazing, but it's just starting to feel a bit claustrophobic. I feel him everywhere when all I used to feel was us."

Walking over to me, Annie put her arms around my shoulders. "What is it Sass? Is there something you're not telling me? What's brought this on? And what's more, if you've got a feeling about something it's usually not far off."

"I don't know Annie, sorry, it's probably just me over-analysing the situation. I didn't mean to alarm you or worry you. If it's all good for you, then it's most likely just me. I'll shake it off. Don't look at me like that, it's fine, I'm just over-cautious and cynical, remember." I hugged her back, laughing, and told her again not to worry.

That night I worked late and heard my phone ringing somewhere near the bar. "Hi my love, what's up?" I said as Annika's name appeared on the small screen.

We started discussing an element of work that had arisen during the day. It struck me that she had begun to question herself.

"I think that sounds perfect Annie, go with it," I responded.

"Ok great, just wasn't too sure - you know getting this close I don't want to make the wrong decision," she explained.

"There is no wrong decision Annie. If that's what you want to do I'll always support you. You know that."

Even Audrey had started playing a role in her self-preservation. The topic changed to a dinner Annie was attending with Audrey the following night.

"Aud said Christian now might be tagging along."

"That wouldn't surprise anyone, there's never Punch without Judy," I replied, starting to feel a bit annoyed that we were back on this topic.

"That's a bit unfair don't you think? They're just great mates which I think is really special for a father and daughter."

Treading carefully I replied, "Oh for sure, you know me Annie, I just like my own space. If it was me I'd be telling my father to maybe get a life of his own, socially that is. You know? Sometimes you just don't want your father hanging around all the time, especially when you're older. I'm just thinking about her, how's she going to find the perfect man when it would appear to be her father!"

"Yeah well not everyone's as strong as you Sass, I think her dad gives her security."

"I'm sure he does and that's marvellous, but a dinner or two on her own wouldn't break her. Anyway, back to what you're going to wear."

"I think I'll stick with the blue number, depending on what Aud ends up with. You know how amazing her outfits can be so I don't want to look like the poor cousin. I think she said her dad was going in white tie. I might check with her, my white dress could work too."

"Why don't you call her and get some confirmations, but you know Annie you'd look stunning in a bathrobe. Anything you wear will never come off as the poor cousin next to Audrey. No offense, but as great as her gigs are she needs them just to get to first base, to be in your team."

She laughs. "You would say that! You're my greatest ambassador."

"No Annie, just stating the obvious. Now give her a call, have an amazing night tomorrow and I'll see you at coffee on Thursday. I want to hear all the goss."

"Righto Sass, love you."

"You too hun, see ya."

I hung up, wondering if this awkward feeling I had about Audrey and her father was nothing more than jealousy. Knowing I'd had Annie to myself over the years maybe meant I couldn't share her with anyone. Her friendship had become a priority to both of us over time and maybe that was the real issue? I shook my head, I knew that was not true. I knew I wasn't like that with friendships, that I was trying to make excuses. The ocean lay deeper than that in me and to feel threatened, which was what one might call it, was really not what I was feeling at all. It was more concern or anxiety. It was like I was on high alert, at some point I was going to have an attack, an accident, an episode.

I flicked on my computer and checked the emails. Sixty-two unread messages from yesterday, probably only two or three important. Delete, respond, ponder but my mind kept wandering to the dinner the following night. Why would he want to attend? Last week they went for Mexican, casual non-eventful Mexican and he turned up there. Footed the bill, much to my objection but it had become so embarrassing I had to give in. Yet it was starting to irritate me as the regularity of it grew. Ann got the most distressed but rather than create a scene she would drop cash into Audrey's bag.

Ironically a message appeared from him, not uncommon as he often forwarded messages from various emails regarding a range of topics. The best ones were articles of general interest. Nothing personal, nothing relative to the restaurant, just links to various items of interest. On one occasion I had mentioned my father-in-law was searching vehemently for the right name for his newest acquisition of some acreage. He was an avid believer in Hypothesis and Socrates and the philosophy of the Greek gods and wanted the property's name to reflect this. I had received from him the following day a fascinating link to an ancient Greek gods website. There were a couple - and only a couple - that my father-in-law had not been aware of, and he was beside himself with this newfound information.

Getting up from my computer, done with constantly considering this man and his intentions, a dark shadow crossed my computer screen and I looked up almost expecting him to be there. He was not and I shook myself at the uneasiness. The bird outside the window flew off. A huge weariness enveloped me and I locked up the shop, heading home to my babies and safety.

Chapter Eleven

The phone was vibrating somewhere. Turning over books and piles of paperwork I finally located it between two books.

"Hello." It was a number I didn't recognise.

"Sasskia Hamilton?"

"Yes, speaking."

"Doctor Otto, Sasskia, from The Royal Hospital. I don't mean to alarm you but we have admitted a patient tonight who's asking after you. Do you know an Annika Osborne?"

Silence. A great silence. I didn't possibly think I could go through this again. I couldn't feel my throat. Can one usually feel their throat? If so why couldn't I? Or maybe you actually can't, maybe you feel your oesophagus? Either way, I couldn't feel my throat or my oesophagus.

"Sasskia, can you confirm you know Annika Osborne?" I was still immobilised. "Sasskia, she is going to be okay, but she needs you."

The sound of a heavenly choir. God I hated this mobile. Releasing the tight hold I thought, "Tomorrow I will upgrade, get a new one." Why was I choking? Oh god, I couldn't stop coughing.

"Are you alright Mrs Hamilton?" There was panic in his voice.

The fear slowly escaped through my nostrils. I felt like a horse.

"Sorry Doctor yes, yes this is Sasskia. What has happened to Annika?"

"She's been hit by a car, I'm afraid it was a hit-and-run but she has just regained consciousness and there seems to be no damage to her head."

Oh shit, here we go again. A car accident. "Are you sure she's going to be okay?"

He said that he would continue on with tests and scans and didn't want to say much more until I came to the hospital.

"Is there anyone else we should be calling?" he asked.

"No Doctor. I'll be there in ten minutes."

Grabbing my keys I took the fire escape, flying down the stairs. Tonight was the dinner - why was she out on the road? What time was it? 11.10pm. Christ, I had no idea it was so late. Where were Audrey and Christian? Oh God, don't let her die.

Running through the hallways I located the area for the operating rooms. The information had been zero from the night receptionist in the main foyer. She was lucky I was so scared or I would have knocked her block off. Taking deep breaths, trying to ignore my rising anxiety I spotted a couple of nurses.

"Excuse me, I'm trying to find Annika Osborne. She was admitted an hour ago in emergency. Doctor Otto?" I asked, growing impatient. Two doors down they pointed, in the direction of the last theatre, the next room up. "Thanks," I bellowed at them, making tracks.

The doctor was sitting on a chair by her bed with a chart in his hand. He was expecting me.

Walking a little more calmly now, I introduced myself. "Sasskia, Doctor - oh, oh um sorry I didn't catch your name," I weakly smiled, knowing I was appearing like a half-wit.

"Otto, Doctor Otto but Oh-oh is fine." He smiled back at me. "Come with me please," he said. "She's asleep and I've told her you're on your way. We'll talk while we walk, if that's ok with you?" Falling into step next to him I waited. "We don't have many details on the hit and run, that's for the police, her condition though is stable as I said over the phone. She has however suffered some serious injuries. Her spine could be a problem. We are waiting on some test results. Her brain and head are fine - the cat-scans are good, all clear. There are no obvious broken bones but her spine as I just mentioned is a concern. The level of severity is still unknown. It could be significant, it could not be. There is a chance - and I need you to be prepared for what I'm going to say: that she may not walk again. It is not at this point confirmed but there's a risk, given the damage to her spine. She knows this, I have spoken with her. I need you to focus on the positives and keep her focused on the positives. Do you understand? She needs you to be a shining light. Unfortunately, we manage the doom all on our own."

Looking at him, the tenderness in his voice, the kindness in his eyes, his quiet pleading for me to be strong to assist him to work alongside him for my best friend was effective. I tried to digest the information. She could be paralysed, my athletic best friend. I had to discard it, what use was I going to be. She had gotten out of much worse in her life, this fighter, this survivor. No, he was right. She needed me to be her partner, confirm her strength. Changing from the woman who entered the hospital to the woman standing outside the hospital door of her best friend I nodded to no one in particular.

"You ready?" he asked.

With a determination that even surprised myself I looked at him; "You can count on me, Doctor, she's the best friend I've ever had. I'll pull her through and that's a promise."

"Wow," he said. "Everyone in this hospital could use one of you. Let's go in."

Chapter Twelve

As Audrey had expected, he was coming. The worst part about it was that she hadn't even invited him. Annika had been talking about it in front of him, assuming he had been coming. The quickness in his reaction didn't surprise her either. He didn't for one minute let on that he was unaware of the Awards night, that he in fact wasn't invited, he simply nodded and agreed that if any was going to win it would be her, his daughter. As he left he had quietly suggested to her that he would like to come. And so it was, he was coming without a further word. She had wanted it to be her and Annika, the anticipation of just the two of them against the world was all that had mattered. The design being judged was from a previous job and she was keen for Annika to see her in a different light.

She wanted to impress her, make her proud and the thought of being totally independent of her family on such an auspicious occasion was liberating. She only really cared about Annika's approval, her support and enthusiasm for her and her work. She knew her family would be happy but it wasn't an engagement, an announcement of a new baby. She had had many female friends before but none like Annika. She made her feel special, unique. Her stunning looks and intelligence, her kindness and honesty, the fact that her father also respected and admired her had made it easier. She was enchanting and loved being around her. She knew that Sass and her were close but she was beginning to believe that what she and Annika had was much more real. They had the same interests, both single, no children, alike in so many ways. Sometimes she would finish Annika's sentences for her, knowing exactly what she was going to say and she had been genuinely pleased to be asked to the Awards night. She had even said she would love to be the 'date' of such a talented designer. Her father seemed equally as fascinated, constantly asking about her, her relationships, her work. Whenever he could he would ask her to invite Annika as their guest. She wondered if he almost preferred Ann to her but then decided at least it wasn't her sister.

She had chosen her outfit carefully. She knew Annika's style and wanted to compliment it. Visually Ann was stunning but she knew that with her hair done, the right makeup and her amazing accessories she could at least pass, standing beside her. She had indulged in a pair of Louis Vuitton heels that had cost a bomb and were so high she had practiced night after night walking in them. Her hair was booked in at Sebastian's, the most exclusive salon in the city, and they were going to do her make up as well. The treadmill she had been running on week after week had paid off – she had lost nine pounds.

As she sat in the salon she sighed only briefly about the addition of her father. She was too excited to get wound up, deciding that if she did win, she'd impress them both - a notion she had given up on with her father until a wedding day. By the time they had finished with her she felt like Cinderella.

Walking in her new heels to the taxi, she gave Annika's address and headed off into the night feeling like a rock star.

"Oh my god, Ann you look absolutely stunning," she gasped as Annika climbed into the taxi.

"Wow, what are you talking about! Look at you," she smiled shyly.

"Well when you're out and about with glamour's like you, you gotta make some effort."

Shaking her head, Annika laughed. "On the contrary, you are one-hundred per cent the show stopper tonight. I love what you've done with your hair, it's much lighter, isn't it?"

"Yep, they suggested some highlights. I feel like a bit of a fraud you know, I'm not exactly your cliché blonde."

"Nonsense, it looks fabulous - you look fabulous! And tonight you are going to win, in fact you already have. You'll be beating those potential husbands off with your MaxMara clutch!"

They rode along chatting like school-girls about the night ahead. When the taxi pulled over, she paid the fare and opened her door, straight into her father.

"Hello you two," he smiled warmly. "Look at my baby girl, Annika have you ever seen such a vision? If only it was a different ceremony." He kissed her on both cheeks and did the same to Annika. She ignored her father's remark and grabbed Annika's hand.

"Let's go in, grab a drink." She didn't wait for him and again tried desperately hard not to let the comment upset her.

"What a superb idea," he agreed, falling into step beside them. "Wait for me, my shout."

Sitting next to Annika she realised it was the happiest she'd felt in years. As the band played, with the stage performance, the noise deafening loud and allowing no conversation, she stole another glance at her friend. She had noticed no one else since they'd arrived, even forgetting her father sitting to her left. The group on stage, an American-Idol style bunch, crooned 'J'taime, j'taime, j'taime' and as she glanced at Annika her heart stopped. Annika, feeling her gaze, gave her a quick wink and turned back. She was paralysed by what she felt. It was not the song of love that bleeped from the stage, it was the thud-thud-thud of her heart that woke her up. The daze she felt she had been existing in for so long was thinning. She steadied herself with the table, resting both her hands in front of her. She could only look straight ahead. She could only pretend to be there, immersed in the onstage performance. She was having trouble breathing as the realisation slowly sunk in. There were tears in her eyes and she didn't know how to blink them away, terrified of what may come with it. She moved her eyes only quickly to her father hoping the reality, the image of him would jolt her back to reality. Her brain was literally spinning out of control, in a swift movement she moved her hands to her head in an attempt to stop the swaying. The performance ended and everyone was up out of their seats, clapping, vigorously applauding, hooting. She had never been so thankful for such a crowded moment in her entire life. Had she been in love with Annika all this time? Is that what had been missing? Was she gay? She knew that if Annika lent over and kissed her now she would want it. She admitted to herself she had wanted it for some time. She cheered as loud as anyone else, for herself, for her knowledge, for her blind love. She clapped and clapped, euphoric that she had been saved, found her destiny, found her happiness, here in this beautiful moment. She was the last one to finally sit, not caring how long she had been out in front, on display, a complete contrast to her previous self. She turned to Annika, who was beaming at her and she knew, she finally knew she had found her soul mate, her future. She winked back and planted a kiss on her cheek.

Chapter Thirteen

She had been totally caught off guard. The night had been so much fun. Everyone in great spirits, the food, wine was exceptional and the entertainment had been outstanding. She knew how much it had meant to Audrey, admittedly not until she actually saw her in the taxi. She had coloured her hair, lost weight - not that she had needed to - and her dress was simply one of the most beautiful garments Annika had ever seen. The champagne colour complimented her skin perfectly and the high neck and low back were breathtaking. The skirt dropped to the ground in flattering layers of tulle and ruching. The detail on the fitted bodice was exquisite and Annika had gasped at the sight of her. She had literally transformed into Cinderella overnight. She was excited like Annika had never seen her before, childlike, charming and Annika had found it infectious. Christian too had been in good humour. She had felt so proud of Audrey, so happy for her, in front of her father until he had made that awful comment. She was regretful that she hadn't defended her, retorted, retaliated. Audrey had handled it perfectly, luckily, and she promised herself she would rally to her defence if he tried to cause any further trouble for the night.

After the band had finished she started overtly antagonising her father and playfully interacting with everyone at the table. Maybe the wine was setting in or the impending award was giving her confidence, but she had become more assertive. She even made a couple of crude jokes that had silenced her father and surprised others. Annika had rather enjoyed the new Audrey, she was far more like Sass – well, more like Sass than Annika was, and she loved her company.

Finally the moment came.

"And the winner for the Young Designer Award goes to… Devan Hope, from Light Blue!"

Even then she remained jovial and happy, congratulating the winner, giving him a hug.

When Christian asked her to dance, she easily accepted. He was a good dancer, not surprisingly, and she felt safe and comfortable with him, her friend's father. He had become somewhat of a father figure to all of them, including Sass, and it wasn't for the first time that night she had wished she was there, her second skin. When they got back from the dance floor she noticed Aud was a bit unsteady, slightly quieter. She didn't have time to enquire as Christian whipped her away, whirling her back on to the dance floor as soon as the next song played out. By now the entire dance floor was covered. Guests were really letting their hair down.

"The atmosphere is fantastic. The few awards nights I've been to have been so boring."

He gestured to the bar, "I agree but I can hardly hear you."

She nodded, relieved for the reprieve on her sore feet and a chance to find Audrey. She saw her in the distance dancing with the winning man and happily thought, "What if tonight turns out to be that as well?" They ventured over to the bar in the adjoining room, the beat of the band disappearing from the room and the new sound of the pianist filling up around the bar. Christian ordered a couple of wines, handing one to her.

"It has been a really good night don't you think?" he asked intently.

"Absolutely, and Aud is in her element. She really is the belle of the ball tonight. You must be so proud. She's a wonderful woman, Christian."

He agreed, nodding his head. "She certainly is. If I didn't know her better I'd think someone slipped her something half way through the night. I've never seen her like that."

"Ah, she's just letting her hair down, Christian, enjoying the moment. It's been a pretty stressful time for her, what with doing our job amongst all the other work she has on. We're not exactly the easiest clients. There's a lot of pressure on her to perform constantly in everything she does."

He looked at her with intensity. "Annika, please. You and Sass are far from difficult. This is the best job she could have hoped for. She copies other people's designs. I'm not saying she isn't talented but she is an interior designer. She looks at the current trends around the globe and applies them. She follows the hot designers and pounces on their new releases. She's not saving lives or inventing - she's not actually even designing, she's copying what other people had the intelligence to create. Don't look at me like that. It's true, it's not bad, it's no problem, she loves doing it but don't be disillusioned to think it's hard and stressful. It's fun and relatively easy and what's more, she gets to see you, almost every day."

He moved in closer to her and swiftly put his hand under her chin, lifting her face to his. Before she could stop what was happening, his other hand was on her back and he was kissing her naturally and confidently like they had done it a hundred times before. She attempted to manoeuvre away from him, gently, not wanting to hurt him and saw Audrey standing behind him, horror spread all over her face. Looking from him to her she was caught. Christian was still only inches away from her and he leant forward again with arrogance and such speed that she was taken yet again by complete surprise.

"I think we are perfect together," he whispered in her ear. "You are beautiful and I can't stop thinking about you."

Audrey turned and ran, catching the tulle of her dress on the corner of the bar, tearing the garment.

"Audrey!" she called, "Audrey, it's not what you think!"

She raced after her, pushing past onlookers. A huge group came through the door laughing and chatting excitedly, obstructing her vision and she lost sight of her, struggling to get through. She stood there, in the main room, searching for her friend, her workmate who she just betrayed - and what's worse, with her own father. Suddenly she felt him, standing next to her.

"What happened? I'm so sorry. I thought you felt it too. Was that Audrey? She won't mind, she knows I haven't been happy in a long time. Annie, Annie, please don't be upset with me. I couldn't bear it. Forgive me. It was the wine, a foolish mistake. I never drink, now I know why. Look at me. Annie, it won't happen again I promise, believe me."

Acknowledging Audrey was not in the room, defeated, she soothed Christian.

"Don't worry Christian, It was nothing, a friendly kiss, a thank you for being such a good friend to your daughter. Think nothing of it, I certainly won't." Patting his arm she broke away. "But now I need to find Aud, I don't think she does understand. The look on her face was not an understanding one."

Christian rang her repeatedly, she didn't answer.

"Let's try out front, the taxi rank, it will take her a while - hopefully she's still in the queue."

Heading out on to the main road they both saw her and Christian leapt out, running towards her. "Audrey," he screamed.

She turned and looked, her face stained with tears, mascara in lines painted down her cheeks. Her dress was a mess, even worse now.

Annika gasped, "Aud, come back, slow down. It's nothing, he was saying thanks," she yelled.

Audrey ran down the street and Annika went after her, the image of her swollen face, her red eyes, her torn dress too much. She slowed at the road, stopped. Annika was just about to touch her, grab her when she took off across the road, narrowly missing the car that Annika never saw.

Chapter Fourteen

The restaurant was flooded by the light of the moon. I turned all the lights off and still the room was aglow. It was ethereal, something I never tired of. Opening the computer I checked my reports, the moonlight comforting, assuring. My husband was always amazed at how efficient I was late at night. He would joke about me being a vampire, equally as evil. It was now that I was reminded of him the most. Midnight, late. I used to get home from work and he would be there, waiting up for me. I always said not to wait up, to go to bed, get as much sleep as he could, knowing the children rose early. He wouldn't have it. He would say I deserved to come home to somebody, working so hard. How ironic, where did that get him? I remember the disappointment I felt with him so often, the feeling of judgement he seemed to leave in the room.

"How did you wash those dishes?" he would accuse.

"Did you scrape the tires on the car?" he would mutter.

"Use soap twice when you wash your hands."

"Should there be more seasoning?" he would doubt.

And on and on it would go. He would tell me I should be more energetic, should be more horny, shouldn't be so tired, shouldn't have had that last glass of wine. There was a novel of shoulds and should nots and Tom was entitled to add or remove from it whenever he saw fit. He was the quintessential Godfather.

"Why do I have to be the bad guy?" he would ask.

"I don't know," I would answer, "I don't know."

Do that, don't do that, eat that, don't eat that, drink that, don't drink that. My life was full of commands. I began to find it hard to trust him. I began to find it hard to like him. He was perfect and I quite simply was not. He was always in total control of everything. That night before he died I had left too. I had gone out looking for myself. Sure I had come home, but had I really? It was only now that I knew I was home, it was only now with him gone that I knew who I was. Now I had no idea.

I stayed longer than necessary in the empty restaurant until it was time to leave. I didn't sleep in my room much anymore, instead opting to bunk in with the kids, hearing his voice up and down our stairs. We had considered selling but it was the children's house too and they wanted to stay, at least until they no longer needed to, which I hoped would be never.

The next morning I read the emails over breakfast. Annika's doctor kept me updated with her progress, which was really quite unnecessary as I was there every day. I think it gave us both some comfort to write things down, achievements, moments. I read his email nearly every morning.

"She will be out tomorrow," he wrote. Why didn't he ring? Reading on, elated, I absorbed the good news. "She had a huge breakthrough during her therapy session late in the afternoon," he wrote. Walking perfectly, almost 100 per cent. I looked at the time, wondering how long I had. "She wanted to keep it a surprise," he explained, "and plans at turning up at the restaurant around noon. Will you be there?" he asked. He would bring her.

I instantly thought about Audrey, knowing I should call her, her vigil as dedicated as mine in the recovery of Annie but it was a long story and still not finished, still no ending, not since the accident anyway. I texted Dr Otto that I would be there. Champagne would be chilling. I threw my children around, telling them the good news.

Driving to work, I wondered about Audrey. The truth was they all had frightened me. I wasn't concerned about Annie, I knew her well enough and knew she would hold her own, but Audrey and Christian and their entire extended family had yet again somehow managed to completely monopolise the situation. Audrey had taken it personally and, like Joan of Arc she had turned into a martyr, taking vigil beside Annie daily.

Annika had walked me through the night of the accident, omitting nothing on the premise that I told absolutely nobody any of it. I agreed; what could I do? But I was shocked and disgusted. I hid my anger and contempt for the whole pathetic family but couldn't shake the feeling that maybe I was responsible too, not paying enough attention to what was going on before our eyes. I had given her my word, I couldn't breathe a word of it to anyone, not a mention of it. What was more, she had concocted a story that I was supposed to relay to everyone, to save their fate, insisting it was actually to hide her guilt at apparently leading him on. She begged me to buy the story, to try somewhere within me to put my feelings aside and not avenge. It started to consume her more than the accident itself and so I had assured her I would keep my word.

They on the other hand had no idea that I knew every finite detail of the night and I hated them for it all. I could barely speak to Audrey in the hospital and if one more bunch of flowers arrived from Christian I was personally going to take them to his office and tell him where to shove them.

I turned the car off in the car park downstairs and melted down. Tom, Annika, not even having Chef Matty around my long term business partner her left me for the new owners, when we sold the last restaurant, felt like a loss. Thierry in Paris, the day-to-day heartache I felt for my children, all these beautiful people imparting themselves on me year after year, their morale's and deep integrity that I admired so much in all of them. Ian, Poppy, my family, Tom's family. Who are these crazy people? How did I end up here with them, after all this?

This toxic family had permeated my life and their façade was still completely intact, untouched, none the wiser no doubt like so many times before. Everyone bowing down to them, this holier than thou family made of deceit, lies and disgust. The accident could have been fucking fatal, a point no one seemed to consider. This family from a hell I didn't know has been spared just because she didn't die. But if that car had been going faster, if Annika had been running at a slightly different angle, if, if, if. They would have paid, been exposed. If he'd put the word on Annika he'd have done it to others before as well, a thought that affected me to the core. I had to think that the accident was the only common ground but I knew it was deeper than that. Audrey now treated me as not so much an enemy, but a threat perhaps, and Annika was like a softly formed stuffed cuddly toy that seemed to be permanently within arm's reach of her. Something further had happened on that night and someone was holding back. I knew Annie had told me all of HER story from the night but something was missing. Why was Audrey so devastated to find her father kissing Annie that she ran out of the Awards night into oncoming traffic? There was something that she was hiding or that Christian and I was determined to know the truth. It bit at me like a vampire, lurching and attacking. I had dealt with enough deceit and treachery; Audrey was not going to be another.

I had every reason to feel such disappointment and a sad pity for them both. Annie had everyone, Audrey had no one. It was unbelievable to me that the latter was calling the shots.

Chapter Fifteen

The morning of the Opening night had arrived. Annika had stayed over.

I arose early to go for a run, everyone still asleep. By the time they stirred I had breakfast ready and espressos waiting.

"So mum, how many magazines will be there?" Grace asked.

"Just the standard local ones, honey."

"How many photos of you will there be?" she continued on.

"None I hope. But you'll see Annie everywhere. She's the real face and I plan on being too busy cleaning up everyone's mess!"

"Gracie, your mum and I will cover every page with our good looks, I'll make sure of it. You'll have something to show your friends. It would be bad form of her not to make an appearance, wouldn't it Gracie?" Annika said, knowing I had every intention of dodging the cameras.

"Honey, it's about showcasing what we do, not who we are," I said, playing along, knowing I would get a photo for her.

The talk was all about the big party that night. I began to relax and started to enjoy the occasion. Annie got up and started clearing the table, the sun shining through the trees that screened my deck from the world outside. I was still amazed that only a month ago there was a chance she would never walk again. Overwhelmed, I jumped up and joined her in the kitchen, giving her a huge hug as she closed the door of the dishwasher.

"What was that for?" she asked quietly.

"For nothing. For being in my kitchen, for being with my family, for doing the washing up, for being in my life."

"Shit Sass, we haven't even had a bubbles yet," she laughed.

"I know! I'm terrified. I'll get it all out now so there's nothing left for tonight. I don't know how I'm going to keep it together!"

Annika smiled, admitting to herself she didn't know how Sass was going to keep it together either.

"But really Annie, it's been a long time since I've felt this happy. It feels like I've got a real partner again, if you know what I mean."

"I take that as a huge compliment Sass, and it's you who deserves the thanks. You already had all of this," she said, sweeping her arms around the room, "I just joined in. You would have been here with or without me but I wouldn't have been. I'd still be working on the island in my little cafe wondering where on earth I was going to end up, wondering if this was me ending up."

"That's rubbish honey, you were tremendously happy when I met you."

"I was in tears by the first night we spoke," she argued.

"We both were, if you recall. That doesn't mean you weren't happy. You were, or we were, finally letting our defences down and talking. Honestly talking about what we'd been through. It's me who was lost and floundering. Sure you weren't doing this but you were doing exactly what you wanted and that was miles from where I was. You brought all this together for me, no one else."

"You're my best friend Sass. You have included me in your family, supported me through the whole accident, kept my story, kept all my secrets! Don't think this was about you. I am a completely different person to the one you met all those years ago and you are solely who I thank for that. There has never been anyone like you in my life and you're my hero, in everything Sass you're my hero."

There were tears rolling down her cheeks and we stood in the kitchen hugging each other. The kids shrugged, having seen it all before, and both came in for the hug too.

"Hey you two," Gracie spoke up confidently just like her mother. "You both saved each other, and us and now we have you both. Tonight will be so cool."

I wanted to capture this moment forever but my mind wandered to that fatal rainy day. It seemed like yesterday and in the same moment a lifetime ago. She hadn't replaced him but she seemed to have made life a little more normal for me without him, more bearable.

There was a knock at the door at the front of the house. Gracie ran to open it and came bounding back down the hallway with the largest bouquet of flowers we'd ever seen. She grabbed the card out of the side of the plastic and read out loud: "Lovely Sass, good luck tonight. You deserve it. Christian and Dorella."

The staff I had were superb and Annika's kitchen team were the best around. Industry professionals had come out of the woodwork and some of the greatest names in the game were now on our payroll. It was three P.M. and everything was going to schedule. The bands were setting up, the kitchen was on target with their prep, all the booze was cold and ready, the glassware had all been polished. The professional cleaners had done such a thorough job that I had asked them to come back at six for a once-over before the guests arrived. Texting Annika to let her know all was going to plan, I left Eloise my ever faithful manager in charge and told her I'd be back at six.

My mum and mother-in-law were both at home when I got there, both of them so important to me. Delighted to see them, I hugged them both tight, always on these kind of occasions a little emotional.

"Everything okay at the restaurant honey?" my mother-in-law Pearl asked.

"Fantastic, it's really going to be great. I can't tell you again Pearl how wonderful you are. Are you so sure you don't want to come? Tom would be so chuffed that you were there." Tears sprang to my eyes, as she held me in her warm embrace.

"Tom would be so chuffed that you're doing this my darling. This is exactly where I want to be - with my babies. Don't be sad Sass, he would be so proud of you, just like his father and I are. You're an amazing mother and an amazing daughter-in-law and I consider you a daughter. Go and enjoy it. Celebrate for Tom, celebrate that these kids have such a great role model in their life. You've pulled yourself through, I never would have. Be proud and, hey, next month we're all off to France to see what you and Thierry have done over there in honour of Tom, just look at all you've done in the last five years. Stand tall Sass, remember these things; life, walking tall, confidence. The sky has cleared, the wind is on your face. The emptiness, the isolation is gone. This is your serenity. Remember him now. He understood you. He knew you, he loved you."

My mum looked fantastic, she was still so beautiful, no wonder my father had fallen for her even until the end. Smiling at me we both walked inside, linking arms. How was it that here we were, the two of us, on our own but with each other. I sensed her moment, the joy and yet the deep sadness. For both of us, for the irony, for the deep losses, for the heartache and the treachery. We couldn't have imagined our fate, we couldn't have imagined this destiny.

When the driver arrived mum and I felt like Cinderella going to the ball and I, frightened, looked around for Poppy. I noticed Pearl checking her phone nervously, wondering also where he might be, knowing I was not leaving without seeing him. She took my hand, both of us knowing what she was feeling, using every survival technique I knew not to crumble. God, oh god don't let anything happen to him, just get him here safe.

Just as the driver started the engine his car pulled up in the driveway. Running down the path, just like the children do he called out to wait. With tears in his eyes he was whispering in my ear how much he loved me. Calmly, as had always been his way, he embraced me, telling me how wonderful I looked and what a beautiful person I was. These wonderful people meant more to me than I had ever realised and I was so grateful in that moment that they entered my life, so grateful they had accepted me as family, nothing changing, even when the world around me was constantly. Like Tom they were my rock now, they were the best of him. They stood beside me, tall and smiling. We had cried and cried and cried, sad cries, all sad cries and now it almost felt like the cloud was lifting.

Mum stood to the side now, knowing how strong the three of us were, had become. The driver beeped the horn lightly, I kissed my beautiful children and took mum's hand. It was time to go, the stage awaited; with a deep breath and Tom in my heart I promised him I would make him proud. Tonight, I said to mum, is for Annika and Tom. She nodded, not safe enough for words.

The room was buzzing when we arrived. People were everywhere. Waiters by the droves, musicians, magicians, models, models posing as actors, the singers. A full symphony orchestra. The landlords had allowed the use of the rooftop exclusively for the night and she was keen to see the final result.

We took the lift to the rooftop. The door slid open and we stood speechless. The transformation was a miracle. The stage for the band was elevated on ten steel poles and sitting on the top was a huge sheet of glass, up-lights changing colours intermittently. The band's instruments were in position, awaiting their arrival, ready to perform, high above the city and the river below. Bonfires glowed around the terrace, emanating soft light. Suspended across the building next door were the two words 'Left Bank', lit up in Moulin Rouge-style lettering so large against the night sky. It was only when I looked closer that I actually saw a series of tightrope bridges that connected all the rooftops together that circled the building. Each rooftop – of which there were four - guests could move around on, had their own set up. The furthest being a cinema lounge where old French movies were being constantly played, intrinsic to the theme of the restaurant. The most exciting rooftop was the haute couture, where a catwalk had been created around the bonfires and through a water feature standing as high as the band's stage to the left. The deck was clear, no one allowed - not even staff - until the exact time. I looked over at Annie who I had kept the details from as we were crossing from bridge to bridge, the effect breathtaking.

"Sass, oh my god this is so stunning. How did you ever think of it? How did you pull it off!"

"The Moulin Rouge movie of course. Everyone roof-hops in Paris, don't you know? I wasn't sure about the streets below under these bridges but it feels amazing," I said, laughing.

"You have outdone yourself. This will be the talk of the town, no, the globe."

"Hopefully, hey, Anne. As long as it puts the restaurant on the map, I don't care who talks about it. I don't want to fail you."

"Christ. I hope my food can live up to this," she muttered.

"Nonsense Annie, it's a couple of bridges."

"Thinking of food is making me feel sick, I think I'm going to throw up I'm so nervous," Annie said, looking very nervous.

"You know love, we just have to smile for a few hours and then leave them to it. Everything's in place. I've got undercover security, police, the works. With our old mate Chef Matty keeping an eye on the kitchen, we are freed up for the night, we'll be fine."

"Yep you're right, don't worry, I'm up for it. Just watch me work that room tonight."

Giggling at the image we headed back to the restaurant level. There were ten minutes left before the guests arrived. We went in opposite directions for one final check and I stopped and took a photo on my phone to send home. The tower clock that we had set up at the entrance to the building chimed, signalling the first arrival. I squeezed Annie's hand, awaited, looked and smiled.

One hour down and the party was shaping up to be a success, chatter and music filled the room. The morning had been spent with the TV crew from Nine Alive, one of the morning shows, broadcasting live from the restaurant. It was like nothing that had been done before. The success of reality TV and the huge phenomenon that it had become had prompted the channel's producer Lowry Farce to seek out new ideas for the station.

Ian's brother was a cameraman for Nine Alive and one morning he had turned up at the restaurant to drop a package off to Ian. His mate, also a cameraman at the television station had tagged along, en route to a corporate Golf Day the station was hosting. The rest had really happened during the tournament. The friend was the producer's nephew and over dinner later that night he had mentioned his mate's brother's latest project, a swanky new restaurant on the city fringe. Lowry had said nothing but turned up himself a week or so later with the idea. The filming was to take place live the morning of opening night, then again the following morning, showing all the apparent highlights and dramas that unfolded, then one week, two weeks and a month later to follow the progress of the restaurant. Apparently ratings had soared that morning for Nine Alive's broadcast and the presenters were here, enjoying their French champagne, patting each other on the back. The phone at the restaurant had been constantly ringing since the show ended and the business computer had crashed, unable to keep up with the website hits emails flooding in. This sort of exposure had the potential to set the restaurant up, providing we kept up our game.

Chatting with the anchors, going over the morning's activities, mum whispered in my ear: "They're here, just wanted to pre-warn you." She squeezed my elbow and moved off in the direction of my sisters.

A couple more TV personalities arrived and they all started to talk amongst themselves.

"Excuse me for a moment if you don't mind. Loved the piece this morning. Well done."

"Hi Aud, enjoying yourself?" I asked, seeking her out.

She was elated, receiving compliments and accolades, securing leads that would put her on the map, and yes, absolutely make her the winner at the awards night next year. As usual Christian was hot on her heels. I glanced around for Dorella. Not surprisingly she was nowhere to be seen, had been nowhere to be seen; after the accident it was as if she simply vanished. She stopped coming to the restaurant and her name was never spoken.

"This is so fantastic Sass. Annika has done an amazing job with the food, everyone is raving. I overheard someone talking about a TV show for her, that's real talent, hey."

"She's remarkable, I agree," instantly realising I disliked her now and maybe always had.

"Have you had the wasabi & sake oyster shots?" I enquired with a forced smile.

"Have I ever. Maybe four already, they are stunning."

As she rabbited on about the food and wine, her sudden knowledge was overwhelming as I felt myself watching her as if from a distance. She was certainly trying hard tonight. One could have mistaken her for genuine and supportive - even Christian looked slightly humble, keeping to the background. Her ideas were fantastic, there was no doubt she had added to our restaurant, she had the creativity but at what price had it come? Watching them mingling on the floor I couldn't wait to be rid of them. There was nothing left in me to give them. It felt like they had drained my soul with so much trickery, so much betrayal and now they were laughing and smiling, freely accepting accolades from admirers, sweeping arm gestures around the room, nodding in the direction of particular items, the water feature, the Eiffel tower structure bar. I knew I should never have gotten involved with them. They were dangerous, like parasites and I knew like parasites they would be hard to shake.

"Snap out of it," I told myself, seeing Nic, one of my oldest friends and her husband Sam waving furiously at me.

"Hey honey, I'm sure you've been hearing it all night but yet again Sass, you've outdone yourself. This is just so incredible! You deserve an Oscar. Tom would love it."

Kissing Nic on the cheek I said, "Thanks my love, but let's not get too ahead of ourselves, it's just a restaurant and hopefully a successful one."

She hugged me. "Everything you do is successful, it's what we love and hate about you."

"Hey, be careful Nic," Sam interrupted, "without her there'd be no 'us'." He was winking at me.

Nodding smugly at Nic I retorted: "That's right girlfriend, be nice to me," remembering the night all too well. We had planned a massive girl's weekend away, set itineraries, booked restaurants, planned our outfits but when the weekend came around it was only Nic and I who had turned up, the others finding it hard to get a leave pass from their partners.

My mind wandered to the night before, we were having a conversation around the dinner table at home and the children were telling me how I used to be always shooting off for a night here and a night there, with the girls. It had really surprised me that they had that impression and when I argued that there had only been a handful, they started to reel off all the occasions. I had to concede that they were right, there wasn't an occasion I missed out on. I had never given Tom any thanks for that – in fact I used to get so upset that he never encouraged it, even though he never discouraged it. I always wanted more. He used to say to me, he had everything he needed here, in this city, in this house. He would say if you need to go, well go and I had, every time, needing it.

Nic was talking about the flight, the worst flight we'd ever been on, on that holiday and we both remembered it. We had headed straight to the airport bar and ordered two rums, drinking them straight and without a word. We had landed, we were lucky and we had managed to get to a booking at the hottest spot for dinner that night. It had happened then during dinner, Nic, after hearing the punchline of some restaurant story I was telling, howled uncontrollably, turning everyone's heads in the very cool and sophisticated dining room. Sam, at dinner with some of his friends, hadn't been able to take his eyes off her after catching sight of her. When we were leaving he had approached calmly and asked us if we'd like to join them for a drink. Nic had declined, explaining we were on a strictly girls' weekend. However, still single and Sam being very good looking, I said yes, we would love to. Nic non-committedly agreed, saying we were on our way out anyway. That had been the beginning of the end. He moved, they were married a year later and now had two beautiful children. He was great for her, the last of my single friends, and Tom and him had connected straight away.

Relieved to have such good old friends, trustworthy and caring, I put my arms around their waists. "I'm so glad you two are here. There are so many faces, so much bullshit, I'm so grateful to see ones I love."

Before I knew it an arm was on my elbow, pulling me firmly around. "Sass you must meet Marc, his TV show has just topped ratings and he is keen to get you and Annika on it."

Turning away from yet another celebrity chef I rolled my eyes at them and winked, mouthing sorry. Nic raised her glass and blew me a kiss, leaving me to it.

The orchestra began playing and everyone quietened down, watching the performance. To the side I noticed Annika and Aud heading to the lift. Ah, good idea, a moment's break while nobody's watching. Excusing myself from the group, I made for the same direction. Eloise grabbed my attention; one of the ovens seemed to be losing heat, anxiously we headed for the kitchen. Unsure of the problem I reset the oven hoping my fail proof strategy concerning mechanics would work, it flashed back on and the temperature started to rise. The chefs went into overdrive madly filling trays, commencing the cooking process again. I loved the kitchen, the pressure. During the whole potential crisis, no one spoke, no one stopped, that's simply the kitchen, it will be fixed, there is food cooking, no one stops.

Pushing through the guests who were fortunately occupied by the orchestra I quickly jumped in the lift, the door closing silently in front of me. It opened again moments later on the rooftop and I gasped, completely taken aback. Neither of them saw me, slightly obscured by the stage. Surprised, I watched Audrey and Annika kissing, or Audrey kissing Annika. Wait, something wasn't right; Annika was awkwardly pushing her, shaking her head from side to side but Audrey had her firm, her hands holding either side of Annika's face. They started to push and shove.

Annika was speaking now, "No, no." She fell backwards and Audrey was instantly on top of her.

"I love you Annie, I always have. I think about you all the time, all day. I know you feel the same. You treat me differently to others, you love me, I know you do."

What the hell? What was happening.

Annika started wincing emotionally in pain, "I don't love you like that Aud, I'm not in love with you. You're a friend, just a friend."

"No, I'm not just a friend!" she screamed at Annika, hissing at her. "I'm going to be your lover, I AM your soul mate, we are soul mates." More gently now: "I've got a huge surprise for you. I've bought us a restaurant. I stole a lot of money from my fiance before I left Korea, he deserved it, you'd be proud of me and with Dad we've bought a building where you can have your own restaurant. We bought it together for you, for us, to go our own way. I told him we were going to be a couple, that we loved each other, that's why you wanted nothing to do with him at the Awards night. He understood, he's so happy for us. You wait, you'll love it, you just have to get used to the idea. But I know you Annie, I know you'll love me." She was pleading with Annika, louder and louder, covering her with her conviction, her helpless assuredness.

"Get off her," I said from behind, moving quickly towards them. "There's a roomful of press downstairs only too keen to hear what you've just said Audrey, the daughter of the distinguished Christian Brown's daughter. Your whole fucking family will be exposed. Now, as I said, get off her."

"Sass? What the fuck are you doing here? God, why are you always around, everywhere I turn? Can't you leave her alone. She loves me Sass, not you, not the perfect miss Sass, the poor beautiful widow, she loves me. Get away from us. Annie my darling, tell her who you love, tell her."

In one fell swoop Annika rolled out from under Audrey and inserted a knee into her back just as she tried to scrabble up from the ground.

With Audrey faced down her head held tight against the concrete roof top Annika spoke. "When I say, you're going to get up," she said slowly. Her voice was a voice I'd never heard before, it stopped me in cold. It was animal, guttural, deep and strong.

"Now, get up you stupid fucking slut and look at me. I don't love you. I don't even like you, you fucking cow. Get your father, your mother, your whole fucking family out of my life. You have completely misread me, Audrey. I've only ever hated one other person in my whole life and I put him behind bars. You don't know a thing about me. I used to be a cop, you idiot. Embezzled money did you say? Did you know it was your mother who was driving the car that hit me? I didn't think so.

"Your dear dad confessed to me in hospital. He told me she was a raging alcoholic, that he can't stand the sight of her, that he's had a thousand affairs. That was his lame excuse, your mother's drinking. Your family and your fucking secrets are pathetic. What's even worse for you Audrey is that I'm an ex cop. How do you feel about jail? I've still got a lot of friends who wanted to get into bed with me, maybe I should call in a favour or two. Now, get out and if you even think about turning around you will regret it until the day I make you die. Don't ever come near me or Sass again. I promise you, you'll regret it!" She grabbed her arm and shoved her toward the lift. "Did you hear me, I use to be a cop you fucking idiot, since you think you know all about me."

She scrambled inside the lift, the door slid across. Annika crumbled to the ground, the tears were streaming down her cheeks.

"How dare she touch me," she whispered, "how dare she touch me."

Holding her still, we were both trembling. "It's going to be alright honey, she's gone, she's not coming back, it's alright. You're safe."

We sat there in silence, like that. Holding each other, like that. Confused, exhausted, blinded. The lift door opened and the band members fell out talking happily amongst each other.

"Are you okay Annie?"

"Yes," she said, "I'll be fine, you go, everyone will be wondering where we are by now. I'll be fine. I just need a few minutes to get myself together."

"Don't rush Annie, I can handle it. You've been through enough. If you want to go, tell me, mum will take you."

"Sass, they are not going to drive me out of tonight too."

"Man, we sure do go through some shit. I mean it though hun, don't rush. I'll make sure they're gone. Take your time."

Back downstairs I looked around nervously, searching people's faces, scanning their outlines. Hurriedly I rushed to the window, the view expansive, hoping I would see them leaving, gone. Walking quickly, a great distance between us, were two figures, black against the night sky, no shadow to be seen. The full moon bore down on them, highlighting their distorted faces, still they walked shadowless. Nothing felt them, nothing followed them. The collar on his jacket pulled up high, shielding him from the stark open empty air, warming him from the narrow, crisp vacancy. Her shoulders were bent, her hands were stuffed in her pockets. She walked straight ahead on the street below. The wind was behind them, propelling them on, away, gone. They grew smaller and smaller, shrinking under the stare of the moon. It turned its back on them too, they shuffled now, feeling the void, sensing the end.

People were talking to me, smiling, laughing, one last look out the window and they had vanished, gone. I turned my back on it, said good night to the moon, my moon, my midnight moon who never failed me.

"Hey Eloise, how's the kitchen? It's time for the supper dishes. Can you bring them out every fifteen from now, like clockwork?"

"Sure Sass, done."

"and in between: palate cleansers, twelve per tray, matched to each guests supper dish."

"You can count on us Sass. We're on it."

My mum appeared at my side almost, just like I needed her

"Annika's just over by Eloise, Sass, do you want me to grab her?" my mum asks her eyes more on Annika than me. "Nah I'll get her on my way to make my opening speech. Love you mum but keep an eye on her over the night, will you?"

"Of course honey. Is everything ok?"

"Yep its great but this is her first time at this sort of thing and you and I both know it's not really her thing. I just dont want her overwhelmed by it all."

"She's a big girl Sass. You're so protective of her. She's a lucky one."

"Thanks mum, I'll find you later."

Now I'm almost running towards the stage after noticing the MC looking around for me. I take the two steps up on to the stage just as the MC introduces me and the crowd start clapping. Holding the microphone I'm just about to start my speech having rehearsed it all week opening with an invitation to our world of magic upstairs when I see him. The sensation that I'm about to faint overcomes me and my legs start to give way. I try really hard to focus on standing but it's impossible, I think I am falling but I can't be sure, the room is spinning furiously around and around. This can not be happening. What is happening? Am I losing my mind? I think I'm actually still speaking, I am saying the words, I can hear my voice. Is it his ghost or am I just mad. Maybe there was something in the coffee?. How is he here? What trick is this? He's thinner, younger. A males voice is talking to me, oh god it's not him talking to me, inside my head is it?

This imaginary image? I can't hear his words but his voice feels familiar. He's taking my hands, prying them off the microphone, he has an arm around me, this is not good? Doctor Otto? Doctor Otto is looking at me, concern spread across his face.

"Sass" he says quietly " Can you hear me? Are you in pain Sass? I need you to respond, nod your head if you can hear me".

I nod as per his instructions and then everything goes black.

Chapter Sixteen

Someone had once said not to love a person who makes life easier on you, who you can fool, can manipulate. Love a person who will love you wholly. Challenge you, make you better, wiser. I sit in the quiet of the restaurant listening to Tom's story after all this time.

Its three days later, I had been whisked away quietly by Doctor Otto before any commotion could happen on opening night. When I passed out, only mum had been watching the rest of the guests had made their way up to the after party on the roof top. The moment now, was remarkable, sitting with Tom, my Tom, the man I had never stopped grieving, the man I had never stopped loving, holding his hand. Tears streaming down both of our faces.

He had seen a photo of me on the morning show, on the television. The Nine Alive TV crew that had planted itself there at the restaurant for a solid week, he had been watching. His memory had returned, come flooding back to him after five long years, when the image of me had been shown on his television. Me, his wife, his real life, his children. It had all come back to him.

He had stopped by the ocean side early in the morning, on his way to organising the new beach house he had just bought. He'd got changed in the car and had gone for a swim. He threw all his personal belongings on the back seat, and ran into the ocean. When he got back to the car, he threw his gear back on and just past the 51 exit sign he notice a hitchhiker and pulled over to pick him up. Andy was his name and he felt like a younger version of Tom. He was interested to know what the lad was up to. All he remembers is pulling out on to the road, Andy saying he was on his way south, very south when the semi appeared out of nowhere on the wrong side of the road headed straight for him.

The next thing he knew he had blood on his head and was pulling himself out of the car. There were flames everywhere, he didnt know how much and didn't want to know so he ran as fast as he could from the car not once stopping. By the time he looked up he had no idea where he was, or who he was. He walked on for some time until he came across a Backpackers. They seemed to be expecting him and he played along. Night after night he remained there keeping to himself. Finally he decided he must have been the person they expected as he had no other theory. They made an arrangement with him because he had arrived with no wallet no money, that he would clean the hostel in exchange for his accommodation. After one year of their arrangement the owners had asked him to be the Manager, a fully paid role. He spent every day hoping he would remember something but slowly realising he would never know the truth about his past. He remembered nothing not the car, not the backpacker he picked up, not his wife and children.

And then I was there, on TV, larger than life, advertising a new restaurant. A reality restaurant show, one week to go. He had fallen down in a heap and cried. For two days he remained in shock hiding in his apartment.. His grief and sadness had overcome him, for what he had lost and what he must have put everyone through. He hadn't been capable of seeing anyone, petrified of what he might find, petrified of what would happen. He tortured himself about disrupting my new life, my successful new restaurant. This glamorous new restaurant, he had seen splashed all over the TV screen. The owners had come concerned that the phones weren't being answered and that their manager had appeared to go missing. When they found him he was mute, rocking with sadness. Slowly he started to speak to tell his story. They decided he had to find me, he knew he had to hold me, touch me again. He had to smell his children, lie down next to them, look into their eyes. The pain in his ears was excruciating as he tried to remember their little voices, listen to their lost lives. He was inconsolable, his beautiful children, the highlight of his every day. What had they gone through? Could they go through this now too? Surely they had been through enough but he couldn't bear the thought of it, of never seeing them again. He was sorry, so sorry but he had to come, it was his family. He hadn't died he hadn't left, he had just been lost, lost for five long years and hopefully, maybe, maybe he could stay?

Epilogue

Remember these things Sass. The knowledge, walking tall, confidant. The sky clearing, the martini, the wind on your face, the sound of the ocean. The emptiness, isolation. Silence, serenity. This was serenity. The sound of the ocean, the wind in your hair. Remember him. He understands you when you thought forever that he didn't. He does, he tries, he is aware, he knows but sometimes you're too hard, too complicated.

Remember Sass, the ring of happiness. No more sorrow, no more self-pity. Stand tall, say less, listen more. Remember you have everything and many have nothing. Move forward happily Sass. You are happy, understand that. He is home, you, are finally home.

www.ingramcontent.com/pod-product-compliance
Lightning Source LLC
Chambersburg PA
CBHW051814020726
47502CB00005B/1452